# OTHER TEAM REAPER THRILLERS

# AFRICAN WHITE

## A TEAM REAPER THRILLER 10

## BRENT TOWNS

WOLFPACK
PUBLISHING
— EST 2013 —

**WOLFPACK PUBLISHING**
— EST 2013 —

Published in the United States by Wolfpack Publishing, Las Vegas

Wolfpack Publishing
6032 Wheat Penny Avenue
Las Vegas, NV 89122

wolfpackpublishing.com

Paperback ISBN: 978-1-64734-494-8
eBook ISBN: 978-1-64734-493-1
Library of Congress Control Number: 2020931576

# AFRICAN WHITE

# FROM THE CIA WORLD
# FACT BOOK

**Nigeria:** Home to Islamic State of Iraq and ash-Sham (ISIS)-West Africa whose aim is to implement ISIS's strict interpretation of Sharia; replace the Nigerian Government with an Islamic state. Based primarily in the north along the border with Niger, with its largest presence in the northeast and the Lake Chad region; targets primarily regional military installations and civilians.

**Nigeria:** A transit point for heroin and cocaine intended for European, East Asian, and North American markets; safe haven for Nigerian narcotraffickers operating worldwide; major money-laundering center; massive corruption and criminal activity.

**South Africa:** transshipment center for heroin, hashish, and cocaine.

*For Sam and Jacob.*

# PROLOGUE

*Gulf of Guinea, Nigerian Coast 1998*

"Let me come with you, papa," Abadi Falomo begged his father. "I'm old enough."

Giwa Falomo looked down at his son and smiled, his straight white teeth shining bright against his smooth dark skin. "My brave boy," he said. "Someone has to stay here and look after your mother and your sister. The man for that job is you."

Abadi looked up at his father. The man was big but solid, and each time he moved his muscles rippled like fluid. "But papa—"

"I have spoken," Giwa said firmly. "One day you will get to go with us, but not today. Now, we must go. The ship will be here soon."

The older Falomo reached down and picked up his AK-47 and rested it upon his shoulder.

Abadi watched on wistfully, wishing that his father would change his mind and let him go to capture the ship which would provide them with much money. But he also knew that his father would never change his mind once it was made up.

"Watch for our return, Abadi," his father said.

"I will, papa."

Abadi watched his father walk away, down the beach toward a battered boat that looked more conditioned to sink than sail. It was a rusted, shit-colored vessel that had seen better days, however, once the twin outboards on the back were started, it would slice through the water like a newer, sleeker craft.

Ten rough and tough looking men waited there for him, all in similar worn clothing, some smoking to pass the time. Each man had worked with Giwa for as long as Abadi could remember. But his father had not always been a pirate. At one point in his life, Giwa had worked in a warehouse in Lagos. The pitiful wages he'd earned there had been barely enough to help his family survive. His life had changed at his chance meeting of a man who had taken one look at the big Nigerian and offered him work that paid more than he could ever dream of.

Six months and two hijackings later, the man had been killed trying to board a German-flagged ship. But Giwa, not intrinsically an opportunist, saw the chance to change his life and grabbed it with both hands. Now he had his own crew.

The Nigerian climbed aboard the boat, his heavily armed crew joining him. In the early days, maybe one or two men at most carried weapons, but the Americans and British had stepped up their naval patrols and were intercepting more and more craft on both sides of the continent.

The mothership pulled away from the shore the ropes on its stern tightening as they took up the slack. Once out in the shipping lanes they would change to the two smaller, faster boarding craft they were towing which now started to move and fall into the bigger craft's wake.

A fly buzzed past Abadi's face and he swatted at it with his hand. The sun was still low in the sky, but the day was already hot. The air felt like it would burn the exposed skin on his arms.

The boy looked on as his father turned and waved to him, long muscular arm moving in a large arc, diminishing in size as they moved further away. Abadi did likewise and waved goodbye. Then his father was gone. Engulfed in an all-consuming ball of orange flame from the AGM-65 Maverick Air to Surface Missile.

The blast wave rolled across the calm waters and onto the beach and seemed to buffet the stunned boy. The sound was almost deafening and Abadi flinched as the thunderclap made his ears ring.

His mouth agape, Abadi tried to reconcile what had just happened to his father. His expression was confused, and he didn't hear the roar of the F-16 Fighting Falcon until it burned low overhead.

Then he saw the two boats emerge past the headland. Small, swift, motorized launches used by American Special Forces. They drove straight for the beach where Abadi stood, their course unwavering.

Around him the cries of alarm grew loud and then came the gunfire from the men left behind to guard the pirate base. The Americans returned their fire and bullets started to fizz through the hot morning air.

A man fell at Abadi's feet, a hole in his head. His eyes were still open, and they peered sightlessly back at the boy who looked down upon him. Beside the dead man was an AK-47. Abadi bent down and picked it up. "I will look after Mama, Papa. You will be proud."

The boy raised the weapon, pointed it at the oncoming craft and squeezed the trigger. The weapon bucked and bounced and sprayed bullets wildly through the air. He fought to correct his aim but by the time he had done so, the magazine was empty.

Abadi frowned wondering why the gun would not fire. He jerked on the trigger time and time again but still nothing happened. The American boats slid onto the yellow sand and the men aboard leaped from them. Gunfire grew in intensity and Abadi threw the AK away, turning to flee as fast as he could. Bullets seemed to be chasing him across the sand as he prayed for his legs to carry him faster. He saw another man die when two bullets from the American shooters hit him in the chest.

Tears of fear and grief started to stream across Abadi's cheeks. "Mama! Mama!" he cried out.

The F-16 thundered overhead once more and a second explosion erupted further inland. A fireball rose above the shanties and Abadi dove to the ground. Suddenly a hand grasped his shirt and a deep voice said, "Get up young, Abadi. Find your mother."

The boy looked at the man who'd dragged him to his feet. He held an AK-47 in his right hand and a bandolier of ammunition crossed his chest. He'd seen him around the beaches before but never knew his name. "Go!" he ordered him. "Go now!"

No sooner had the words escaped the man's lips when his chest seemed to explode, the shirt he wore now a shredded mess of red. Abadi started running again trying to get away from the chaos. He reached the first row of shanties and slipped between two corrugated iron abodes. Another explosion rocked the area, closer this time.

Abadi burst from between the structures and almost ran into an American soldier. The man reached out for the boy, but he deftly stepped aside and kept running.

"Hey, kid, get back here," the soldier called after him.

Abadi's heart felt as though it was about to burst but he was nearly home. He would get his mother and his sister, and they would leave. Telling her about his father would have to wait.

Behind him the gunfire seemed to be never ending. He ducked once more between two structures. He was close now, almost home.

When Abadi burst clear of the narrow alley he stopped dead, his eyes looking about crazily for his home. What he took in before him was a blackened, burning crater in the ground. His heart was in his mouth as he stood there, stunned at the realization that his family was all gone.

# CHAPTER 1

*Cardoso, Mexico*
*Present Day*

Walking out the door of his rundown adobe style home, Mayor Fernando Ibarra put his head up and sniffed, his olfactory sense detecting an unmistakable smell. The air was thick with fumes of petroleum fuel and he knew instantly what was happening. For years now, the cartels had been tapping into the underground petroleum pipes, siphoning off tanker loads of fuel each time. The work was extremely dangerous, but the payoff was far more lucrative than drugs.

The fumes hung on the slight breeze blowing throughout Cardoso, its narrow streets shrouded in an invisible mist. Ibarra coughed. "Idiotas estupidos," he growled and began walking along the dust-covered street towards the edge of the town.

This had happened numerous times before, and the mayor wasn't happy that it was happening again. The first time the cartels had done it, they had left the tap point in the pipe exposed. The petroleum company had then come along afterwards and resealed everything, covering the pipeline over. The next night the cartel people returned with a digger and tapped the pipeline six feet away from the previous breach.

It was a common occurrence in the current climate. In 2001, detected illegal taps numbered just over one-hundred and thirty. In 2018, they registered twelve and a half thousand. The driving force behind the dramatic rise was one Amaya Caro. Known throughout Mexico as La Vibora, or The Viper.

Her father, Manuel Caro, had been leader of the Durango Cartel, a small operation back in the day when the cartels respected and stuck to activities within their borders. He was known as La serpiente de cascabel or The Rattlesnake.

However, as times changed, the larger cartels began weeding out and taking over the smaller ones. But Manuel Caro was tenacious and would not be forced out, clinging to what he believed was rightfully his. He armed his men with modern weapons and fought back. Then one night in two-thousand and nine a rival, The Pantera cartel, performed a hit on his small motorcade, killing everyone present, including Caro himself.

Without a head on the snake the Panteras figured the Durango Cartel to be a pushover and began preparing for a takeover. The one factor they hadn't allowed for was Caro's daughter, Amaya. Although considered young at the time, in her early twenties, Amaya was her father's daughter and had been a part of his operation from an early age, and was totally capable and prepared to do everything necessary to enforce her authority upon the cartel itself.

Word had it that during her period of mourning, just three nights after her father's demise, she had summoned his six lieutenants to a meeting. During a dinner of celebrating the life of her father, drinking and toasting his memory, a man slipped into the room with an automatic weapon and shot them where they sat. He was known only as The American. An assassin hired specifically because he was an outsider and there was no one within her father's organization she could trust.

After having cleaned house, people began to sit up and take her seriously. But Amaya wasn't done yet. She used The American as her weapon of choice and he bludgeoned his way through her rivals. Within a year, she held territory from Durango through to Mexico City. Along the way she had gained the name of The Viper. Now apparently, she was preparing to expand once more with The American clearing the path before her.

As Ibarra grew closer to the edge of town the smell of petroleum fuel was almost overpowering. People started to run past him with plastic containers in their hands. "Fools," he grunted. Then he shouted, "You are all fools!"

One of the passersby turned but never slowed. "Hurry, Fernando, get some petroleum for yourself. Before the company comes to fix it."

As he reached the edge of the town, what he saw astounded him. There had to be at least sixty of his people there all trying to capitalize on their good fortune.

The earthmoving machine that had been used to excavate the hole to get at the pipeline was still there, parked off to one side. He recognized it immediately as one of the ones from further along the road where a culvert was being replaced after the last one was washed out.

"Get away from it, you fools!" Ibarra shouted at them. "Do you realize how dangerous this is?"

No one listened to him. They were beyond reason. And why not? They lived in a poor town with little money to keep them going. When they did have money, it went to the cartels or the corrupt police for "protection". The cartel protected them against the police and the police protected them from the cartel. Either way the citizens of Cardoso were left with virtually nothing. In this life, whatever little they could get for free was a godsend.

When he reached the point adjacent to where the gathering of townsfolk was siphoning the fuel, what he saw raised his sense of alarm. Not only were the fumes stronger still, but the hole which had been dug was half full of petroleum and the people were just scooping it out with whatever manner of container they had.

The mayor's blood ran cold and his dark hair almost turned white on the spot. He could feel his heart beating in his thick chest and then the overwhelming urge to run away. This was bad. No, it was worse than bad. It was—

The explosion was massive, like someone had dropped a hundred bombs upon the small town. Those who were closest to the pipeline were completely incinerated. People further away turned instantly to blackened, charred lumps of meat and would only ever be identified by DNA.

However, the devastation wasn't contained to only one area. The fumes that had blanketed the town, ignited too like a rolling carpet of fire. The flames leaped through the air and swallowed Cardoso like a huge fire-breathing dragon totally unprepared to show any mercy.

Once the fumes had burned off, the town itself was left a smoldering wreck. Screams of the burned and dying echoed along the narrow main street which only minutes before Mayor Fernando Ibarra had walked.

When the final tally was made, there were one-hundred and forty dead and the small town of Cardoso ceased to exist.

### Lagos, Nigeria

DEA agents Paul Fritz and Mike Shane studied the intel they'd just received, their visages mirroring each other, concern giving way to anger. "If this is right there'll be hell to pay," Shane, the older of the two said.

Fritz rubbed a hand through his brown hair and stared over at his partner. "Are they expecting us to go up there and have a look?"

"That's what the email says," the broader Shane confirmed. Both men were over six-foot-tall but Fritz was a lot slimmer.

"Jesus Christ it's the middle of fucking ISWA

territory." ISWA stood for Islamic State in West Africa, previously known as Boko Haram.

"Well, according to the intel, they're the ones with the cocaine."

"Why couldn't they just stick to kidnappings and bombings?" Fritz growled.

"If I had to hazard a guess, I might suggest that they're running short on money."

"Shit. I'll be glad to get out of this damned cesspit," Fritz stated. "Two weeks. Two more fucking weeks and I'm gone."

"You want a beer?" Shane asked.

"Sure. Why not? It's certainly hot enough," Fritz said, pointing at the small fan on the table. "That's doing fuck all. You think the DEA could have sprung for a safehouse with air-conditioning instead of this dump."

Shane walked over to the refrigerator and opened the door. He grabbed two bottles of beer, running the cold glass of one over his hot forehead before cracking the lids. Then he took them back to the table and sat down. "This new guy that ISWA has leading them is interesting. He seems to have come from nowhere. I talked to a friend at the CIA and they've never heard of him."

"What did you say his name was?"

"Abadi Falomo."

"That's him. Let's hope we don't get to meet

him personally," said Fritz.

Shane nodded. "I'll organize an escort with Captain Nenge for tomorrow and a plane to Maiduguri."

"I still don't like it. What does the intel say?"

"Just that there's meant to be a shipment of cocaine that has been dropped into the lap of ISWA."

Fritz frowned. "I don't get it. Why would ISWA get a load of coke when they're miles from fucking anywhere? It doesn't make sense. They're not even near a damned port to ship it out of the country."

"I guess we'll find out when we head up country and start asking questions."

"It's still a fucked idea."

"I don't make the rules, I just follow orders."

### *Maiduguri, Nigeria*

Fritz and Shane climbed down from the battered DC-3 onto the red-dirt airstrip outside of Maiduguri. They were accompanied by six Nigerian soldiers, each armed with Heckler and Koch G3s, as their escort. Waiting for them beside the strip were two white Toyota SUVs which were their mode of transport into the Nigerian wilds. Shane said, "At least they look to be a bit better than this rattling piece of shit we just got out of."

Fritz nodded. "Uh-huh. We work for the US government and they supply us with shit like that."

Both men were dressed in tactical gear and armed with M4 carbines and Beretta handguns; all the equipment they would need for their drive up to Gajiram where they planned to meet a contact who had the intel they required.

Shane noticed the gathered soldiers talking amongst themselves, a couple of whom were more animated than the others. "What's going on with them?" he asked Fritz.

"No idea," he replied. "Something has them edgy."

"Let's find out."

They walked over to their escort and Shane singled out the biggest soldier there. "What's going on, Gbayi?"

"They don't want to go any further. They say it is madness."

"Why?"

"ISWA attacked a patrol yesterday near Gajiram. They killed ten soldiers. They don't want to die"

Shane grew angry. "Neither do we but we're going. Now tell them to cowboy the fuck up and get their asses in the vehicles."

Gbayi snapped orders at the others who turned to stare angrily at Shane and Fritz. Shane wasn't having any of it. "You heard the man. Get the fuck in the SUVs."

They scowled at the DEA man some more before grudgingly doing as they were told. Gbayi and another soldier joined Shane and Fritz in the lead vehicle, Gbayi drove. Moments later, the airstrip was receding from view behind them as they drove deeper into the unknown.

# CHAPTER 2

*Team Reaper, Outback Australia*

John "Reaper" Kane climbed the big red sand hill and dropped down beside Cara who studied the compound before them on the flat, brush-speckled plain. "Is that our target?" he asked her.

Dark-haired Cara Billings, callsign Reaper Two, gave a slight nod without taking her eye away from the scope mounted atop her M1A1 CSASS sniper system. "Looks like it."

Kane raised his binoculars to study the scene before him. A large man who topped out at six-four, with broad-shoulders and black hair, Reaper had gained his handle from the grim reaper tattoo on his back. A fly buzzed close to his mouth, seeking the moisture of the orifice, and he blew his breath out savagely, swatting it with his left hand. "Man, this place has so many flies it's starting to drive me crazy." The pesky creature was persistent and unperturbed by the big man's attempts to keep it at bay.

"Don't forget the snakes," Axel 'Axe' Burton said as he crawled in beside his commanding officer. "Australia has something like six or seven of the top ten fucking deadliest snakes in the world. Not to mention, Crocodiles, jellyfish, little fuckers called the blue-ringed octopus. Oh, and don't get me started on this blasted sand. Have you felt how hot it is? This place is just a walking deathtrap."

Axe, like Cara, was a team sniper, but Cara filled the role more frequently than the ex-recon marine. She'd been a sheriff's deputy in another life, and before that, a marine lieutenant. Like Kane and Axe she was in her thirties, but unlike them, she had a slimmer, more athletic build.

Axe on the other hand was solid, taller, relatively good looking, and rough around the edges. What you saw was what you got with him.

"You finished?" asked Cara as she glanced sideways at him.

"Yes, ma'am."

Behind them and standing at the base of the sand hill were the remaining two members of their team. A Former Mexican Special Forces officer, Carlos Arenas, and their combat medic and former navy SEAL, Richard 'Brick' Peters. Both were men of unique skill and experience which had them ideally suited to the missions the team was tasked to carry out.

The five of them had been dropped into the desert the previous evening. It had been cool then, almost cold. But with the coming of the dawn came the heat, and being summertime in the southern hemisphere, the Australian Outback quickly became like an oven.

Kane pushed his soft-brimmed Boonie Cover back and pressed the talk button on his comms. "Zero? This is Reaper One, copy? Over."

Zero was the callsign for Luis Ferrero, the team's operations officer who'd originally put the team itself together. But after their first mission together, changes had been made, and Team Bravo along with Team Reaper, now worked under the auspices of 'The Worldwide Drug Initiative'.

"Copy, Reaper One."

"We've reached the target, will wait for dark before we infill."

"Good copy, Reaper One. Keep us up to date."

"Roger that. One out."

Kane looked at his watch. According to Australian time there was still five hours to go until dark. He asked Cara, "You want to take first watch?"

"Sure, seeing as I'm already here. You figure the target is still there?"

Kane put his binoculars up to his eyes again. "Maybe. We'll find out tonight. I guess."

The target Cara was talking about was Benito Losa. He'd been the head of the Marinas Cartel out of Brazil. He was thought to have been killed in a drone strike in twenty-seventeen but two weeks ago he'd popped up on a small store security feed and been identified by Australian Intelligence. Instead of taking the killer off the map themselves they'd called in The Worldwide Drug Initiative for the job. Losa was wanted internationally for assassinations, drug running, arms dealing, and people trafficking.

After the attempt on his life he'd obviously gone to ground, hence the assumption that he was dead. Apparently, all the intelligence sources were wrong, and he'd continued to manage his criminal empire from the back of beyond, the last place anybody would ever look for him.

But he had been too complacent and stuffed up. Now Team Reaper almost at his door and were about to come knocking.

On the perimeter, Kane counted four guards armed with automatic weapons. "You count four rovers?" he asked Cara.

"Five," she countered.

"Five," Axe confirmed.

"Where?"

"In the shade of the water tank," Cara told him.

The Team Reaper commander shifted his gaze steadily past the house to a large galvanized steel water tank sitting atop a heavy log tank stand, and peered into the shadows, locating the extra guard. The man was dressed in dark clothes which helped him blend into his dark background. "Got him."

"Reaper we've got a dust cloud to the east," Cara warned him.

Kane looked in that direction and picked it out the approaching plume. He couldn't see what was at the base, but knew that it had to be a vehicle coming their way. "Bravo Four, are you getting this?"

Bravo Four was Sam 'Slick' Swift, the team's computer tech who could hack anything, if it had a chip in it, even a toilet.

"Copy, Reaper One, give me a moment."

Kane said into his comms. "Carlos, Brick, get up here."

They climbed the sand hill and lay prone next to the others, their Heckler and Hoch 416s ready to use if necessary.

"What's up?" Brick asked in his low voice.

Kane turned his head in the ex-SEAL's direction. He noted the thin layer of sweat which covered the man's forehead and guessed the rest of his shaved head would be the same. "We've got incoming to the east."

Brick scratched his beard. "Has Slick got eyes on?"

"We'll know shortly."

"What do you want us to do, amigo?" Arenas asked.

"We'll just sit tight for the moment."

"Reaper One, copy?"

"Read you Lima Charlie, Bravo Four."

"ISR shows the incoming contact to be a police vehicle, Reaper. Has to be the cop from Maryvale."

Maryvale was a small one-horse town five klicks east. "Copy," Kane acknowledged.

They watched and waited. The dust cloud grew larger until the vehicle appeared. A white Toyota SUV with a light bar and the word Police on the side. It stopped outside the compound and waited for admission at the razor wire-topped gates. One of the guards let the cop through who drove forward with a start and he pulled up outside the homestead.

"Reaper I have eyes on the target," Cara said calmly. "Steps of the main house."

Kane shifted his binoculars and focused them on the man standing on the wooden veranda just above the steps. Although the distance between the dune and the house was five hundred meters, he was still able to make out the figure of Losa leaning on the brown balustrade. "Zero, confirm the package is on site."

"Good copy, Reaper One. The package is on site."

The police officer and Losa shook hands and disappeared inside the house. Axe said, "At least we know why there's been no sign of him before now. He's got the law in his pocket."

"See that dry creek bed to the west?" Kane asked his team.

They looked in the direction that he was indicating and saw the steep-sided cut running through the plain. At one point it passed reasonably close to the compound. On its banks were a few straggly gum trees and larger rocks. Kane continued, "We can use that to get in close to the compound. Cara, you be good setup here?"

"It's about the only decent high ground around so it'll have to do. I have a reasonably good field of vision, though."

"Reaper," Brick said, "if he has five guards on duty at one time, we can almost count on him having at least five or ten more that we don't see."

"I was thinking that."

"So, this guy is just hiding out and running his cartel from here," Brick commented. "And all the while we thought it was his lieutenant."

"Looks that way," Kane allowed. He rolled over onto his back, placed his 416 across his chest, and pulled his Boonie down over his face.

"What are you doing, Reaper?" Axe asked.

"I'm going to get some sleep. You should too. You're next watch."

The outback sun went away in a bright red and pink sunset and took with it the broiling heat. Kane and the others checked that their weapons were clear of grit before moving out towards the dry creek bed. Each of them wore night vision which turned their world into a green haze. Also attached to their weapons were laser sights that when coupled with the NVGs reached out like lances across the ground to their intended targets.

Their rubber-soled boots crunched on gravel as they climbed down into the dry creek bed. In the distance the howl of a dingo split the night. The path through the creek bed was rocky and uneven. It twisted and turned until eventually it came adjacent to the compound where Losa was hidden away.

The policeman had taken his leave just around dusk, so there would be no issue from that quarter. However, the information they had would be passed along to the federal authorities for them to deal with.

Before Kane led the team out of the creek bed, he pressed his transmit button and spoke in a soft voice. "Reaper Two, sitrep?"

"You have two guards on the west side of the compound close to where you want to breach," Cara informed him. "The other two are over on the south side."

"Can you reach out and touch them both?"

"Just say when."

"Give us a minute," Kane said and turned to Axe and Brick. "There's two guards against this fence. Time to go to work. Hold your fire until I have the command."

"Roger that."

The pair disappeared over the lip of the creek bed and a minute later Axe's whisper came through Kane's comms. "Three and Five in position."

"OK. On my mark. Cara ready?"

"Ready."

"All right. Three, two, one, execute! Execute! Execute!"

There was a long pause before Cara's voice came back to him. "Two down south side."

"Two down west side," Axe informed him.

Satisfied, Kane said, "Push forward and cut the fence, we'll be right behind you."

He crawled up over the lip with Arenas behind him. When he reached the fence, he found Axe and Brick cutting their way through. Just inside the perimeter wire on the right he saw the two lumps which had once been the guards.

Brick worked swiftly cutting with the wire cutters until there was a hole big enough for them to get through.

Once inside they silently walked towards the main house. When he was almost there, Kane and the others dropped to their knees behind an old water trough. "Cara, cover the bunkhouse."

"Roger."

"Brick, Carlos around the back. Axe and I will take the front door. Go in soft. If the shit hits the fan, we Charlie Mike until we get it done. I'll give you a minute to get into position."

The two operators disappeared around the house as they were swallowed by the dark.

"Axe, once we breach, we're going to need

to move fast. We wrap Losa up and call in the Black Hawk for extract."

"Let's do it."

Thirty seconds later Brick and Arenas were in position ready to breach. Suddenly Kane said into his comms. "Abort! Abort! Regroup on me."

"What the fuck, Reaper?" Axe whispered.

"Just do it. Follow me."

### Aboard Skyhawk One, Sixty Kilometers South

The C-17 did lazy figure-eights at thirty-six thousand feet as it held station. Inside the cargo bay General Mary Thurston lifted her head and gave Luis Ferrero an urgent look. "What's going on?" the former Ranger commander asked. She was in her early forties but looked younger. She was athletic, had long dark hair and was attractive to go with it. The clothes she'd chosen to wear for the mission were desert BDUs.

Ferrero on the other hand was in his late forties with graying hair. He shrugged. "Reaper One, sitrep?"

"Wait One, Zero."

Thurston turned to Swift who sat at his console with his computer. "Slick, do you see anything from that satellite?"

The red-headed computer tech shook his head. "I've got four tangos down, Reaper Two is still in position and One through Four are regrouping for some reason that I can't see."

Although not currently concerned, Thurston was still curious as to why an operator like Kane would abort the mission when he was already so far into it."

She looked about the aircraft. Sitting against the fuselage behind her, listening to the radio transmissions were the three remaining members of Bravo Team. Brooke Reynolds was Bravo One. She was the resident UAV pilot. Tall, athletic, long black hair, and capable when the chips were down.

Beside her was the other half of the UAV team. Pete Teller. Formerly a Master Sergeant in the USAF. Beside him sat Pete Traynor. He was an ex-DEA undercover operator. Which was how he had acquired most of his tattoos.

She could see that they too were confused about the turn the mission had just taken.

"Copy, Zero?"

Thurston turned back and looked at Ferrero. "Good copy, Reaper One."

"The doors on the house are reinforced steel. There's no way we're getting through them in a hurry. It'll take too long."

"Copy. Are you aborting the whole mission,

Reaper One?"

"Negative, Zero. We just need to work out how to get in there another way. And fast. Standby."

"Roger that. Standing by."

Thurston's gaze grew angry. "Why don't they have something to breach that damned door?"

"They figured that it would just be a standard door. No one foresaw that it would be reinforced steel."

"Piss poor planning, Luis. Damned piss poor. What was Kane thinking?"

"I don't know but whatever it was, I guess he won't do it again."

**Team Reaper, Outback Australia**

"Sorry guys I fucked up," Kane growled.

"That don't get us inside though, does it," Axe pointed out. "Stop beating yourself up. Mama will do that when we return to base. What we need to do is figure out a way to get in there."

"The way I see it," said Brick, "is we can try and blow our way in with what little grenades we have or maybe hot wire one of their vehicles and smash our way in."

Kane shook his head. "There is no guarantee

that either of those options will be particularly successful."

"Then we make him come to us," Arenas said. "The house is made of wood. It should burn well."

"I agree," Kane said. "Axe get us something to light a fire with. Fast."

"Roger that."

"The rest of you take up security just in case we get rolled before he gets back. Cara, you copy?"

"Copy, Reaper."

"We're going to try something. You'll need to lock the bunkhouse down hard when this kicks off."

"Got it."

A couple of minutes later Axe returned with a small container. The smell of gas was powerful, and Kane said, "Where did you get that?"

"I'm nothing if not resourceful, compadre."

"Then get your resources together and start a damned fire."

Soon flames were licking hungrily at the painted weatherboards, seeking to quickly devour the feast of dry wood that had been served up. Before long the fire had doubled in size, rising to the eaves and spreading outward from the original ignition point. A shout from within indicated that the fire had been discovered, and was only a matter of time before the show started.

The front door flew open, slamming back into the front siding with a loud bang, and an armed man filled the doorway. "Hold your fire. We want them out in the open," whispered Kane.

One turned into three. From inside the bunkhouse another shouted alarm rang out. The door to that opened and the figure who filled the opening was thrust back inside as though by an invisible hand. So too the second who took his place.

It was then that the three men who'd emerged from the house, came to the realization that something was terribly wrong. "Go! Go! Go!" Kane barked into his comms.

Four shooters materialized from the darkness taking the three criminals by surprise. One with a handgun in his fist tried to bring it into line and shoot Arenas but the Mexican was too fast, putting him down with two rounds to the chest.

"Drop the weapons!"

"Get down! Get down!"

The shouted instructions were ignored, and one of the two remaining men raised his weapon, intending to shoot Axe. "Mistake motherfucker," the ex-recon marine hissed through clenched teeth as he fired his 416.

The remaining man didn't repeat his partner's futile action but stood rock still while the team closed in to secure him. "Brick, Carlos cover the bunk house until we're ready for exfil."

"Roger."

Kane pulled his flashlight and shone it in their prisoner's face. The man flinched at the sudden brightness, but the Team Reaper commander held his head still in his grip. He grunted in satisfaction. "Zero, this is Reaper One. Mardi Gras is in custody, I say again, Mardi Gras is in custody. We're ready for extract. Making for the LZ."

"Good copy, Reaper One. See you when you get home."

"Everybody on me, we're making for the LZ. Cara keep our friends nailed down tight until we swing by."

"Roger that, Reaper."

"A walk in the park, Reaper," Axe said to his friend. "Couldn't have gone easier."

"Will you shut the fuck up?" Brick growled.

"What?" Axe asked surprised at the ex-SEAL's reprimand.

"I'm with him," Arenas said.

"Reaper One, this is Bravo Four, copy?"

Kane rolled his eyes. "Good copy, Bravo Four."

"ISR is picking up two fast-moving signatures headed your way from the east. Looks like two SUVs."

"Copy, Bravo Four," Kane acknowledged. Then he turned to look at Axe. "You and your fucking big mouth."

"What? It ain't my fault."

"Alright, saddle up. Double time. Carlos you're in charge of the package. Move now. Cara we're coming to you. Direct route."

"Roger that."

# CHAPTER 3

They jogged across the rough desert terrain.
Brick was rear security while just in front of
him, Arenas was pushing the Brazilian Losa
along ahead of him. The team were hooked
into the same channel, ensuring that any com-
munications that came over the net was heard
by all. The only exception would be a channel
change should it be requested. Each member
heard Swift come back to inform them that the
SUVs were only one mike out.

Headlights bounced wildly as the two vehicles sped over the rough gravel road. Kane said
into his comms, "Cara time to go. Join on us."

The SUVs reached the compound, skidding
to a stop and throwing up a cloud of dust that
quickly washed over them. Loud voices carried through the crisp desert night air. "Reaper. They're some kind of paramilitary outfit,"

Cara told him.

Kane's mind whirled. What the hell would a bunch of militia be doing all the way out here? Behind him, Arenas stumbled, and Losa, not missing an opportunity to try and escape, broke away and began heading in the direction of the dry creek bed.

"Shit!" he heard Brick curse and turned to see the Brazilian making a break for it.

Kane brought his 416 around and squeezed off a long burst. The red earth of the desert exploded around Losa's feet like small volcanic eruptions. He stopped suddenly and remained rigidly still.

"You're not going anywhere, asshole," growled Kane, angry that he had been forced to fire and that his shots had just given away their position. "Carlos, secure him. Axe, keep moving."

They moved briskly past Kane who remained where he was, turning to face the compound in the hope of gaining some insight as to what was happening back there. Bright floodlights lit the night sky, followed by the arcs of singular powerful beams that swept out across the void towards the fleeing team. "Everyone, get down!" The team dove to the ground.

Kane felt the heat of the long-gone sun still

retained by the sand. His heart beat strongly in his chest and the sound of blood rushed through his ears. He waited for a shouted alarm. For gunfire to ring out. Nothing came.

"Reaper One, you need to move," Swift's voice told him. "You've got at least ten shooters in a line abreast walking a search pattern towards your current position."

"Tell me why the fuck do we have militia out here, Bravo Four?"

"No idea, Reaper."

"Then who the fuck are they?" he whispered harshly. "And how did they get out here so damned quick? Someone had to have damned well tipped them off. Shit."

"Argue about this later, Reaper One," Ferrero's voice cut in. "Now, move your ass."

"This isn't over."

"I don't expect it is."

The peaceful night sky was rent by sudden gunfire as bullets whipped low overhead. Kane came to his feet in a low crouch. "Move it people."

Ahead of him he noticed the rest of his team do the same. Their trail took them between stunted trees and clumps of thin-bladed grass. A startled Gray Kangaroo bounded from its shelter beneath some brush and almost knocked Axe off his feet. "Told you this place was dangerous. If it ain't the bullets, it's the damned wildlife."

Cara joined them a hundred meters further on. "Did they see you?"

"I don't think so; they're shooting to see if they can get a reaction."

"Well, let's hope they don't get lucky," she said.

Just ahead the ground dipped, providing shelter for the team from the wild gunfire. Kane turned them right and kept them pushing hard. The ground rose once more, and Kane called for them to pause.

"Where are they at, Bravo Four?"

"They're right behind you, Reaper One."

"How can they be, they can't even see—" his voice stopped. "Swift are you able to pick up any electronic transmissions coming from within our perimeter?"

There was a moment of silence and Kane imagined the redhead's fingers dancing across his keyboard in an erratic rhythm. Then, "Reaper, you're right. I'm picking up a transmission emanating from right on top of you."

"Shit," Kane cursed. "Form a fucking perimeter. The prick is wearing a tracker."

There was a scramble as the Team took up positions. Kane hurried across to the Brazilian and demanded, "Where is it?"

"Where is what?" Losa asked, feigning inno-
cence.

"The tracker, asshole."

Losa gave Kane a winning smile and pointed at his right thigh. "It is there."

"Thank you," Kane said, bringing down his
Ka-Bar knife into yielding flesh.

The incoming fire laid down by the militia
filled the air with angry lead hornets. Along
the perimeter established by the small team
they maintained a strict fire discipline aimed
at conserving their ammunition.

"Are you done yet?" Axe shouted over at
Kane.

Kane, hands bloody from exploring the
wound he had opened in the man's thigh in
search of the tracker, looked up and called
back, "Not yet."

"I told you that you should have let me do it,"
Brick reiterated.

"It'd be fine if this bastard would stay still,"
Kane retorted.

Losa bucked and squirmed in agony at the
intense pain being inflicted on his leg, and
even though Kane had a knee on the Brazilian's chest to restrict him, it wasn't working
out too well. "Fuck it," Kane snapped, lashing

out with a heavy punch to the side of the cartel man's jaw, resulting in the instant cessation of movement.

He felt the tug of a bullet as it picked at his Boonie Cover. Ignoring it, he continued to fumble around in the ragged wound until he felt something hard and small. He extracted it and threw it as far away from them as he could. "I've got it out. Get ready to fall back."

"About damned time," Axe said.

"Brick bring me a field dressing."

The combat medic moved briskly from his perimeter position to where Kane was hovering over the inert Brazilian. "Just cover the wound and give him a shot of something to kill anything that may start an infection."

"What did you do to him?"

"Popped him one. Should have done that to start with."

"Ya think?"

A slug burrowed into the sand beside them. Kane snatched up his HK with blood-coated fingers. "Just get him the fuck ready to go. I've had enough of this shit."

The Team Reaper commander joined Cara in a prone position, and through his NVGs could pick out the militia men's firing positions. "Once Brick is done, we'll be out of here."

"You OK?"

"I'm fine," he replied, firing a couple of shots at a muzzle flash at their eleven o'clock.

"What about our friend back there?"

"He'll live, I think."

"Reaper, I'm done here," Brick said over his comms.

"Copy," came his acknowledgment of the transmission. "Bravo Four, we need a way home."

"Your northwest looks clear, Reaper One."

"Roger that. All Reaper elements head to your northwest," Kane ordered. "Let's move."

"What about Laso?" Brick asked.

"Is he awake?"

"Yes."

"Then he can walk. Move out."


"How are we looking, Bravo Four?" Kane asked twenty minutes later, convinced that they had lost their tail.

"ISR has you clear, Reaper One. The tangos have pushed east."

"Roger that," Kane acknowledged and then said into his mic, "Taipan One-One this is Reaper One, come in, over."

"Reaper One, this is Taipan One-One. Read you five by five, over," came the pilot's voice, heavy with an Australian accent.

"Copy, Taipan. We're good for extract. Will turn on our strobes to mark our position."

"Roger that, Reaper One. Taipan inbound."

Kane turned to his team. "Get your lights on. The Black Hawk is inbound."

For a while the night was filled only with the sounds of nature, but the serenity was soon shattered by the whop-whop of the helicopter's blades as it began to reach out across the star-filled outback sky, steadily growing in intensity until Kane could pick out the flashing lights on it through his NVGs.

"Reaper One, this is Taipan One-One. We have visual, will be touching down in two mikes."

"Roger, Taipan."

The Black Hawk's approach was steady until it flared and then touched down, its rotor wash sending clouds of dirt and debris flying, desert sandblasting exposed skin. The team rushed forward. Cara, the first one to the helicopter, counted them off as they climbed aboard. Five out, six in. "All accounted for, Reaper."

Kane nodded. "Taipan One-One, we're all accounted for. Let's go home."

"Copy, Reaper One. Taipan One-One coming out."

The Black Hawk came clear of the desert floor, lifted into the air and powered away.

### Gajiram, Nigeria

Shane, Fritz, and the Nigerian soldiers waited for two days in Gajiram until their contact finally showed. On more than one occasion the DEA agents discussed getting the hell out and were about to do just that when contact was made.

On a crossroads in the middle of nowhere they met him at a roughly-constructed mud hut surrounded by tall dry grass.

The name of their contact was Akunna; a slim man whose garb amounted to little more than rags. He was already present at the meeting point when the two white SUVs arrived.

Both Shane and Fritz climbed from their vehicle and approached the man while the Nigerian soldiers formed a small perimeter. The DEA agents shook hands with their contact as Mike introduced them to him. "I'm Shane," he said. "This here is Fritz."

"My name is Akunna," the Nigerian said in heavily-accented English.

"What do you have for us?"

"Not out here," the man said. "They have eyes everywhere."

"You mean ISWA?"

The nervous-looking man nodded.

Shane indicated to the hut, looking around the surrounding landscape. "In there?"

"Yes."

They followed him into the small abode, ducking their heads at the low door clearance, and their nostrils were immediately assaulted by the stench of stale animal piss and shit. Fritz wrinkled his nose, but Shane ignored it. He was more interested in what Akunna knew. "We're here, now talk."

"ISWA have a load of drugs, cocaine I think, which came in three weeks ago."

"How do you know this?"

"I saw them unloading it."

"How the fuck would you get close enough to see them unloading it?" Fritz asked with a derisive snort.

"You think I not tell the truth?" Akunna asked him testily.

"I think you're full of shit."

Shane held up his hand. "Just hold on a moment, Paul. Give him a chance. If he's talking shit, he don't get paid. What else did you see?"

"Men in suits."

"What do you mean in suits?"

"Yellow suits."

"Come on, Shane," Fritz growled. "Let's go. He's yanking your dick."

Shane ignored his partner. "What kind of

yellow suits?"

"I have seen them before. In the Congo."

Suddenly the air inside the hut grew stuffy and a sense of dread swept over Shane. He reached into his pocket for his cell. No signal. Fuck. "Describe the suits."

"They were yellow and had a hood," Akunna explained simply.

"How many had them?"

"Two of them."

"Two of who? Were they ISWA?"

Akunna shook his head. "They had skin the color of you."

Shane looked at Fritz. "What do you think?"

"I say he's full of shit."

Shane nodded. "Maybe." He looked at Akunna. "Where were they?"

"Baga."

"Now I know he full of shit," Fritz growled.

Baga was a town in northern Nigeria near Lake Chad. It had shot to infamy after an attack by Boko Haram in twenty-fifteen. Between the 3rd and 7th of January, a series of mass killings had taken place in which it was reported that somewhere between one-hundred and fifty to two thousand people were killed or missing. But 'who to believe' was anyone's guess, with the reports varying greatly between the western and local media.

The terrorist target had been a military base which consisted of troops from Niger, Chad, and Nigeria.

"Pay the man, Paul."

"You're kidding. He's given us –"

"Pay him," Shane said abruptly.

"You aren't thinking of doing what I think you are?"

"We need to find out what Falomo is up to," Shane told him.

"We're not the CIA, Shane. Call them and let them do the dangerous shit."

"We're here, Paul. So, we may as well go and have a look. Besides I don't have any reception."

"We have the damned sat phone, Mike. Call someone and hand it off."

Shane considered the request and then nodded. "OK. Take our friend here and pay him. I'll call someone I know at Langley."

*Langley, Virginia*
*7:10 am*

The phone on Melissa Smith's desk rang twice before she reached for the receiver to answer it. "Yes?"

"There is a call for you from Nigeria, ma'am," the secretary's voice said on the other end.

"Who is it?"

"He said his name was Mike Shane."

"Put him through."

A few seconds later a distant voice came through the handset. "Melissa?"

"Mike? Long time no see. How are you?"

"I've been better. You still dressing it up for those knobs in Washington?"

She turned and looked into the glass of her window. She was in her late thirties with long black hair and a tall, slim build which turned most heads when she walked along the many corridors of power in Washington. "You know me, Mike. I try to make an impression wherever I go."

"I bet you do."

"What can I do for you?"

"I have a bit of a problem."

"Do tell."

"Paul Fritz and I left Lagos the other day and headed up to Borno State to meet an informant."

Melissa turned her chair back to her desk and leaned forward. "Shit, Mike. What are you doing in the middle of ISWA country?"

"Like I said, we got a call from an informant who believes that ISWA had a shipment of cocaine."

"Let them keep it, they might OD on it," Melissa said. "Get out of there."

"Can't. We've turned up something else. Our informant told us that ISWA had two white men there as well when he saw them unloading the coke. He said they were wearing biohazard suits."

"Where?"

"Baga."

"Christ. What do you want me to do?"

"I need a team. We've got Nigerian soldiers who are unreliable at best. An armed escort would be good."

"I don't have anything in Nigeria at the moment. Call it a day, Mike. Turn around and head back to Lagos."

Shane's voice was determined. "Can't do that. We need to see what they're up to with that coke."

"You'll go up there alone?"

"If I have to."

Melissa sighed. "Can you lay low for a couple of days, Mike?"

"Sure."

"All right, I'll have a team out from Incirlik with a biohazard guy. It'll take a couple of days. Give me your coordinates."

"Thanks, Melissa."

"Yeah."

*Incirlik Airbase, Turkey*

The sat phone rang and rang before First Sergeant Ward Solomon answered it. At first, he was hoping it would go away but knew that if he didn't answer it a pile of shit would fall upon him from dizzying heights above. He eased Specialist Mary Crane away from him and climbed off his bunk.

She rolled over to watch him, the thin sheet falling away to reveal heavy breasts. "Let it ring, Ward. We haven't finished yet."

"Don't worry," the big, blond-headed Delta operator said. "I'll be back."

He picked up the sat phone and hit the answer button. "Yeah?"

"Ward, it's Melissa. I have a job for you and your team."

He gave a heavy sigh.

"Interrupt something did I?" the CIA director asked.

"Maybe."

"She'll have to wait for the moment."

"Where are we going?"

"Nigeria, Borno State."

"That's hip-deep in shit, Melissa."

"It is," she allowed. "There are two DEA people there who have stumbled onto something. It might not be much, but on the other hand it could very well be something. I'm going to send a biohazard expert with you."

Solomon frowned. During his years as an operator for Delta and the CIA he'd been a lot of places and seen a lot of things, but when the director calls you personally and mentions the word biohazard, all indications are that it's going to be bad.

"Anything specific I need to know about this op, Melissa?"

"I'm not sure. All I know is what I've been told. It's more of a look-see mission. Get in, get the intel, and get out. You've got a couple of days to be in-country. I'll send you everything before you leave."

"Copy that."

Solomon hung up and walked back over to his bunk. He looked down at Crane and said, "Move over."

# CHAPTER 4

*The worldwide Drug Initiative HQ*
*El Paso, Texas*

… and although the authorities down here in Mexico are no closer to working out what happened, it is believed that the explosion was caused by one of the many illegal taps which the cartels are currently using to steal petroleum fuel…

"That's bad," Cara said to Kane as she entered the rec room. "So many dead."

Kane looked over at her as she sat down on the sofa across from him. She was wearing sweatpants and a green T-shirt. He was dressed in his usual jeans and a blue shirt. Noticing the can of beer in her hand, he asked, "Where's mine?"

"Didn't get you one, sweetie, sorry."

"Where're the rest of the team?"

"Axe and Brick are in the gym and Carlos is in the kitchen, cooking us a meal."

"Really?"

"Uh-huh. He's whipping up some fancy Mexican dish. He did say what it was, but I can't remember the name of it." She took a swig of her beer and held it up. "You want some?"

Kane nodded. "Sure."

Cara threw the beer across the gap between them and he caught it in his right hand, spilling nothing. Kane took a drink. It was cold, tasted good.

"You figure the Mexican government will do anything about this?" she asked, indicating the television.

"They're stretched beyond anything they're capable of at the moment," Kane replied. "They seem to be paddling like hell and going no-where."

"Word is that Amaya Caro is behind this tap."

"Who told you that?"

"Our local super sleuth," Cara replied.

"Slick?"

"Uh-huh."

"Where would he find out?"

Cara smiled. "Ve haf our vays."

"Shit. If he said it then I'd say it is true. She's

the driving force behind everything down there, at the moment."

Cara chuckled, leaning toward him to take back her beer.

Kane shook his head, took another swig on the can before saying, "I wish they'd let us go after her."

"Can't do that without the Mexican government asking us, you know that."

"We could go in dark. Wouldn't be the first time."

"But it won't be this time," Thurston said as she walked through the doorway. Behind her were Ferrero, Axe, Brick, and Arenas. Bringing up the rear was a man in a suit who was carrying a clipboard in his right hand. With a frown, Kane glanced at Cara who mirrored his facial expression.

"Everybody, take a seat," the general ordered.

The attendees quickly found places to sit except for the suit. Once they were settled Thurston turned to indicate the stranger. "This is Mark Fredricks from the Justice Department. He's here to get some facts on record about our last op in Australia."

"Why?" Cara asked.

"A complaint was received about a specific event, and he has been dispatched post-haste to investigate it."

Axe put up his hand. "Ma'am, is he cleared to hear what we have to say?"

The black-haired Fredricks cleared his throat and said, "I can assure you that I'm cleared to hear all you have to tell me."

"Didn't ask you, asshole. I asked my commanding officer."

"Take it easy, Axel. No need for the hostilities."

Axe ignored the use of his full name and bulldozed on. "From what I can gather, General, is that Mister Suit here is here on a witch hunt. Am I right, Mister Suit?"

"I'm just here for the facts," Fredricks stated.

"Who exactly is under investigation?" Ferrero asked.

"The team as a whole, but Mister Kane in particular. The complaint focusses mostly on his actions."

"Let me guess," said Brick. "Laso, right?"

"I'm not at liberty to say."

"The fuck you aren't," Axe growled. "Do you have any idea what we do? What we go through every time we go downrange in the name of justice?"

"I'm sure you do a lot of—"

Without allowing the man to finish, Axe bulldozed his way through, determined to bring some awareness to this ignorant fool. "We've all been wounded at some stage. Cara died twice on one mission until she was brought back, same with Brick, me, Traynor. We've all bled for the cause, for our country, Mister Fredericks. If you have a problem with any of our actions, then take it up with the cartels. We just deal out what they deserve."

"All right, that's enough. I have assured Mister Fredricks that we are willing to assist him in every way possible. Now, that's all."

"You heard the general," Kane said aloud. "If you are asked questions, then you answer them. Tell the truth and it'll be all good. Who do you want to start with, Fredericks?"

The man looked at his clipboard. "Who's Axel Burton?"

Axe stood up, looking down at the man in his suit. "That would be me."

Fredricks nodded resignedly. "It would be."

Reynolds poked her head through the doorway and said, "Sorry, General. There's a call for you."

"I'll be right there, Brooke."

"Yes, ma'am."

Thurston turned her gaze on Fredricks. "You'd best get started, Mister Fredricks. Understand this, however, your investigation does not fuck with my team. They have a job to do, let them do it."

"I assure you, General Thurston, I also have a job to do."

"We'll see," she grunted then turned to Axe. "Play nice with the man, Axel. Or you'll have me to deal with."

"Yes, mama."


Thurston picked up the handset, hit the button, and said, "Thurston."

"Hello, Mary, it's Hank Jones."

"What can I do for you, General?"

"What's going on, Mary. Why so short?"

General Hank Jones was the Chairman of The Joint Chiefs and a close friend of Thurston's. He was also her direct boss. The only one above him was President Jack Carter. The big man bore a striking resemblance to General Norman Schwarzkopf. "I'm sorry, Hank. We've got some guy here from the Department of Justice investigating what happened on our last mission."

"Ah, yes."

Thurston's voice grew cold. "You knew about this, sir?"

"I might have heard something about it."

"Christ, General, can't you get rid of this guy? Reaper did the only thing he could have at the time. The team was about to be surrounded. His only option was to remove the tracker."

"By stabbing Laso with a knife?"

"He's damned lucky I wasn't on the ground with them. I'd have put a bullet in his head and left his ass there."

"I believe you would have," Jones said. "Anyway, I didn't call to argue with you. I have a little something for you to do."

"Fill me in, Hank."

"It's about this terrible turn of events in Mexico."

"The petroleum pipeline explosion?"

"Yes. The Mexican government has reached out to us and asked for our assistance with it."

"How exactly?" Thurston asked.

"Take the team down there, find out what happened, and go after those responsible."

"What help will we get from the Mexican government, Hank?"

"They will have a small force of specialists who will assist you from within their military," Jones explained. "Have you heard of Los Escorpiones?"

"The Scorpions?"

"That's them. They're an elite unit within the Mexican Special Forces."

"Can't say as I have."

"Ask Carlos, I'm sure he'll be happy to fill

you in on some details."

"Yes, sir."

"However, the Mexicans have made a couple of stipulations about you being on the ground."

"Oh yes?" Thurston said, sounding suspicious.

"No UAVs are to be flown in their airspace, and you are to share command of the force with their representative."

"Who is he?"

"She. Her name is Flavia Ojeda," Jones explained. "She's from the CNI."

"Mexican intelligence?"

"That's the one. Is this going to be an issue, Mary?"

"It'll be fine, sir. When do we go?"

"Tomorrow."

"I see," she said a little apprehensively.

"What is it?"

"The matter of our friend from Justice."

"Take him with you. Let him see what you do. Maybe it'll turn out favorably for the investigation."

"Or he'll get shot," Thurston added.

"Then your problem will be solved, won't it? Let me know if you need anything. Good luck, Mary."

"Thank you, sir."

She left her office and found Ferrero talking

to Fredricks. Axe was waiting impatiently on one of the sofas in the rec room. "Sorry to interrupt, Luis but we have an operation. We leave for Mexico tomorrow."

"Hold on a moment," Fredricks blustered. "I still have an investigation to complete."

"As you shall, Mister Fredricks," Thurston told him. "You're coming with us."

"No, I'm not."

"If you have any desire to complete your investigation, you will. Besides, it'll be the perfect opportunity for you to witness first-hand exactly what it is we do."

"What's going on, Mary?" Ferrero asked her.

"The Mexican Government asked for our help with this fuel situation. We'll be working with one of their elite units. Plus, I'll be sharing command with one of theirs."

"Not ideal."

"No, but we'll work with it. Get everyone up and about. It's time to go to work."

"What about me?" Fredricks asked.

Thurston looked him up and down doubtfully. "Can you shoot?"

"A little."

She said to Ferrero, "Get him a gun and a vest. Just a handgun, not a 416."

"I'll see to it."

With a nod, Thurston called over to Axe.

"Your lucky day today, Axel. Join the rest of the team, we're getting ready for a mission."

"Yes," the ex-recon marine said joyfully. "What about the questions?"

"Mister Fredricks has decided to grace us with his presence on this one. While we're deployed, he'll be your responsibility. Keep him alive."

"Do I have to?"

"Look after him or keep him alive?"

"Both."

"Just make sure he comes back home, Axel."

"Yes, ma'am."

### Gajiram, Nigeria

It took a day and a half for the small CIA team to turn up. Half a day early which was good for the DEA men and Nigerian soldiers waiting for them. Ward Solomon introduced his team; Truck, a large man with short black hair, a thin tough-looking shooter named Homer, and another with red hair had the handle Turbo. And the biohazard specialist, Ben Grady. It was late in the afternoon when Mike Shane briefed them on what he knew. "ISWA has a camp somewhere up here near Baga. That's where my source saw the people in the biohazard suits."

"We're in Africa; there could be any number of reasons why two men were wearing biohazard suits," Grady said. "Ebola for instance."

Shane stared at the well-tanned face on the middle-aged man. He considered the answer for a moment and then said, "Normally I would agree with you, but Ebola hasn't been heard of in Nigeria since twenty-fourteen. And there is the fact that they were white and in the company of terrorists. Which is why we need to check it out. They had a lot of cocaine up there and they don't need suits to move that shit."

"So, what then?" Grady asked.

"We could stand around here contemplating it forever," Solomon said. "But that ain't going to get it done."

"That's about it," Shane agreed. "We need to get up there and have a look."

Solomon nodded. "We'll leave after dark. It'll be safer traveling that way. Can we trust your Nigerian soldiers?"

"Just about as far as you could kick Mount Rushmore," Shane said. "Oh, they're good people on the ground, but if the shit hits the fan they aren't going to stand."

"Let's have a look at that map of yours again," Solomon said.

Shane moved to position it in front of the Delta man so it could be clearly seen. Solomon stabbed at the map with his finger. "If we leave the vehicles here and recon on foot from there."

"That's about twenty or so klicks into the target area," Fritz pointed out.

"If Falomo gets wind of our presence, the vehicles aren't going to do us any favors. If we leave them and walk in, there's a greater chance that we remain undetected."

"What if they discover us?" Fritz asked. "We've got no quick way of getting out of there."

"Then we fight like hell and pray for the best."

"I don't like it," Fritz protested.

Solomon nodded. "Neither do I and if this was all about the drugs, I'd tell you all where to get off. But from what you've told me it isn't, and we need to check it out. All you have to do now is convince your Nigerian friends to come along."

*Ovarro City, Mexico*

Ovarro was northwest of Mexico City. When Team Reaper arrived, the city was dark, and the orange streetlamps gave the streets an eerie atmosphere. Many of the buildings passed by the convoy of Humvees, had a tag in some form on them identifying the territory of the cartel in control of the region. That particular cartel belonged to Anaya Caro. Following the four Humvees was a large, black, eighteen-wheeler truck, carrying most of the teams' required equipment.

Arriving at their destination at a little after nine in the evening, their base had previously been a school, built in a flat-sided U-shape, abandoned some two years ago. The small convoy passed through a set of iron gates and pulled up in a large courtyard. Behind them the gates were closed, and when they alighted from their vehicles, Kane looked around, quickly noticing the snipers on the rooftops.

A dark-haired woman in her thirties, approached to greet them. She was wearing a suit with a vest over the top of it. She held her hand out to Thurston. "I'm Flavia Ojeda. It is a pleasure to meet you, General Thurston. I look forward to working with you."

"Likewise," Thurston nodded. She indicated Ferrero. "This is Luis, he's my field supervisor."

"Pleased to meet you," Ojeda said, taking his hand.

"You too, ma'am."

A man dressed in tactical gear joined them and Ojeda introduced him. His name was Domingo Cruz, he was a captain in the Mexican military and the commander of the Scorpions.

Thurston sought out Kane and called him over. "This is Captain Cruz. He's commander of our partner forces. Captain, this is Gunnery Sergeant John Kane; he's my field commander."

Each man gripped a hand with the other, sizing each other up and down, noticing that they were built to a similar standard, one slightly taller than the other. They shook hands. "Pleased to meet you, Captain."

"Call me Domingo, or Cruz. We are not so formal here."

Kane nodded. "Call me Kane or Reaper."

"Reaper?" Cruz asked, cocking an eyebrow.

"Long story."

"How about we all get settled in," suggested Flavia. "Then tomorrow we shall go and observe the site of the latest incident."

Thurston nodded. "That sounds good to me."

"If you are hungry there is food at the cantina. We opened it to feed all of the people."

"Did I hear someone mention food?" Axe asked, holding Fredricks up with one hand.

"Get the gear unpacked first, Axe," Ferrero said. "Then you can fill the damned cavern in your face."

"Yes, sir."

Once settled in, the team went into the canteen and ate their fill. After supper, Kane and

Cara took a walk up onto the roof where they could look out across the city. In the darkness it resembled a Christmas tree with all its different colors.

"It looks so pretty," Cara said. "If you didn't know what lay beneath—"

Her words were interrupted by the distant pop-pop of small arms fire. It was followed by an orange flare of an explosion, standing out like a beacon against the darkened backdrop.

"You were saying?" Kane asked.

"It is a regular occurrence in the city of a night," Cruz informed them as he walked up behind them, coming to stop at the edge of the rooftop. He held up a handheld radio and switched it on. Through the static Kane and Cara could hear the alarmed chatter and the gunfire. The Scorpion commander said, "It is a small police patrol. They are being attacked by some members of the Durango Cartel. They are calling for help, but by the time it arrives they will be all dead."

"Why don't we roll out?" Cara asked.

"It would make no difference."

"And things like this happen most every night?" Kane asked, incredulous.

Cruz nodded. "Cartel violence, yes."

"What do you and your team do amongst all of this?" Cara asked, suspecting that the question would make the captain defensive.

"We fight a losing battle. But we fight it any-way."

"What can you tell me about Amaya Caro?" Kane inquired.

"Ah, yes. La Vibora. She is a deadly one. She took over running the cartel from her father after he was murdered. With the help of one man she had all of his lieutenants killed before they could attempt to make a claim for the chair at the head of the table."

"One man?" Cara asked.

"Yes. A Sicario called The American."

"Who is this American?" Kane queried.

"An assassin whom Amaya Caro wields like a sword. Once he was for anyone to hire. But now he is loyal to only one. It is said that he shares her bed at her bidding. From what I have learned from prisoners we have questioned, he used to be an American soldier."

"Do you have a picture of him?"

Cruz shook his head. "He always wears a hood to conceal his identity. But one day we will know who he is. That will be the day he will be at my feet with a bullet in his head."

"Maybe that day won't be too far away," Kane offered.

"I hope so."

The trio stood silently watching the lights

of the city for several moments. It wasn't long before the sound of gunfire returned.

### Durango City, Mexico

It was a two-story mansion constructed of yellow sandstone set amid lush gardens complete with a large inground pool and no less than six water features. The driveway was paved and led up to a turnaround with a marble fountain set as its central feature. On either side of the house were double garages. With one on the right and two on the left, there was secure parking for six vehicles.

The interior of the home consisted of a large master suite with an extravagant bathroom, a fully equipped gym with circuit training machines, two expansive living rooms, a dining room with a table that seated twelve, and many other areas that remained unused by Amaya Caro.

Her current location inside the well-lit mansion was the gym where she was four kilometers into her ten-kilometer run, part of the fitness regime she performed most days of the week, and the reason her figure resembled that of an athlete's than a normal woman in her early thirties. Muscles rippled across her torso with each movement, made visible by the black sports crop she wore. Her dark hair was pulled back in a ponytail and bounced in rhythm with her taut buttocks each time her feet pounded the treadmill.

Just outside the glass doors to the gym was a single-lane indoor pool which was utilized by Amaya, swimming countless laps after her workouts in the gym. By that time, it was usually about midnight and her normal routine was to finish the night with a drink and then sleep in her king-sized bed. Preferably not alone because The American should be back soon from Mexico City where he was taking care of some business for her. The small matter of a government minister caught taking more than he should. A transgression that he would pay for dearly, not only with his life, but that of his family.

Amaya felt a tingling in her nipples pushing hard against the fabric of her top as they hardened. She always had such a rush of desire when The American was taking care of business for her. Being the wielder of such power; having life or death firmly in her hands and not just at her fingertips, was the ultimate aphrodisiac.

"Are you nearly finished?" the voice cut across her reverie. A broad-shouldered man with dark hair stood in the gym's doorway.

Amaya felt her pulse quicken. She tried not

to let her desire show but the man could read her like a book. It was her one weakness, and she had already decided that if at any time in the future should it become too overwhelming, she would have him killed. For the moment, she was happy to maintain the status quo. She came off the treadmill, a sheen of sweat covering her forehead and cheeks. The American noticed the hardened nipples trying to burst from her top, and smiled. "You been thinking of me again, Senorita?"

"Always," she said, coming close to him. She stared into his brown eyes and traced her finger along the scar on his right jawline. "Swim with me." It was more a command than a request.

"I have something to discuss with you," he told her.

"No, Mark. We swim, then screw, then talk."

Mark Franks recognized the look in her eyes and understood that to stand between Amaya and her desires was perilous at best. But there was something she needed to know, and he wasn't about to let it slide just yet.

"We need to talk now, Amaya."

She stared at him, her dark eyes sparking. Who was he to defy her so openly? When she had used him all those years ago, he'd been a lost soul. A killer without a purpose. She, Amaya Caro, had returned purpose to his life. Upon leaving the U.S. Army after a second deployment tour of Afghanistan, Franks had wandered aimlessly through the first six months of his afterlife, before coming across Amaya and her subsequent request that he kill for her.

He'd been about to walk away when she'd made him a very hard to refuse offer of one-hundred thousand dollars. Franks had paused only momentarily before accepting. During that brief contemplation, he thought about how he'd killed in Afghanistan, so what would be different? In reality the difference was vast. Killing for the cartel was violent and bloody and unforgiving.

"What is so urgent?" Amaya snapped.

"While I was in Mexico City, I learned that the government has invited American Special Forces below the border to help fight the cartels. They have teamed up with Los Escorpiones."

"So what?"

"They are in Ovarro City to help with the petroleum theft. And to target you specifically."

The news made Amaya pause to consider what she'd just been told. "Then you must go and welcome them. Take some of my soldados to help."

"As you wish," Franks said.

"Good, now that is settled, we swim."

The American nodded. "We swim."

# CHAPTER 5

*Borno State, Nigeria*

The early morning sun in Nigeria was just waking up. However, the men who walked through the sparse bush of Borno State had been doing so for the past eight hours. So far everything had gone to plan. But things have a habit of going wrong when you least expect it. And that happened when one of the Nigerian soldiers disappeared off rear guard.

"We need to turn and go back," Fritz stated. "Anything could have happened to the man."

"We need to find him," Gbayi said to Shane.

"What we need to do is locate the camp and see what Falomo is up to," Shane growled. He could already feel the sweat rolling down his back again. The day promised to be another cooker.

It was Solomon who came up with an idea. "How about we push north from here and circle around a bit before coming back onto our original heading? I figure half a day should put us where we want to be."

"Sounds good to me," Shane agreed. "How about you, Fritz?"

"It hasn't sounded good to me since we left, but what the hell? I'm in."

Solomon stared at the Nigerian. "Well?"

He nodded. "I still don't like leaving my man—"

"Your man ain't coming back, Gbayi. He's either taken off of his own accord or ISWA has him. Now, if it is a case of the second option, then we need to set a new course."

They all agreed and pushed north for another couple of hours before hooking back to the right towards their original destination. Turbo walked rear guard with another of the Nigerians, to keep an eye on him lest he was to disappear like his comrade.

It was an hour after that last course change that they cut their first sign of trouble. Although what they found was only a couple of boot prints, it was sufficient to cause the group concern.

"This changes things," Solomon said to Shane. "Delta Team, set up a perimeter. Doc, you stay low where you are."

"What do you suggest we do?" the DEA agent asked the Delta operator.

"The way I see it, we have two options," Solomon informed him. After a momentary pause he said, "No, make that three. One, we can keep going and hope for the best. Two, we can say fuck it and turn around to go back, or three, we can wait for dark and continue that way."

Shane thought for a moment and said, "We wait for dark."

Solomon looked at Fritz who also nodded. The Delta man said, "OK then. We wait for dark."

"We've got company," Truck's voice came over the comms. "To the east. I can see the bastards creeping in using the low ground."

"Same this side too, Ward," Homer called in.

"I guess our decision has been made for us," Solomon said. "Prepare for contact."

Everyone took cover behind whatever they could find. Solomon and Shane were side-by-side. "You see them, Shane?"

"Yeah," Shane replied. There were about twenty men out in the sparse scrub, coming toward them, low, weapons ready.

"Ward, they've got us surrounded," Turbo said over the comms.

"I figured as much. No prizes for guessing who they are. Get ready," Solomon said and brought up his FN-SCAR ready to engage. He turned to Shane. "Don't let these fuckers take you alive. You don't want to end up as headlines on MSNBC."

"How about we kill them all and we go home?" Shane shot back at him.

Solomon nodded and grinned. "I like that idea."

When it kicked off it did so slowly. At first there was just one shot. It was followed by a lengthy silence then another two. Then four, then seven, then Solomon and his men opened fire.

Professionals that they were, they spaced their shots, picking targets to make sure their bullets weren't wasted. Fritz and Shane tried to copy what they were doing but the overwhelming urge to put more outgoing fire into the attackers took over.

The Nigerian soldiers on the other hand burned through their ammunition like fire through tinder-dry grass.

Shane fired three times at an ISWA fighter and saw him fall and not move. One of the man's friends tried to drag his body into cover but Solomon shot him, and he fell atop his prone comrade. The air above them was alive with incoming fire. Bullets snapped loudly as they passed close. The odds were high that someone in the group of friendlies was bound to take a bullet and that person happened to be Gbayi. A slug hit him high in the chest. He cried out and Shane glanced in his direction. He saw the Nigerian soldier sprawled on the ground his weapon next to his outstretched right arm.

"Shit," he hissed and turned back, letting loose half a magazine in a heartbeat.

"Easy, Shane," Solomon cautioned him. "Use it wisely."

The DEA agent did as advised. He dropped out the expended magazine and slapped a fresh one home. He then began to space his shots.

"Ward, we're about to be overrun on this side," Turbo's voice sounded steady as he informed his commander of their diabolical predicament.

"On my way, Turbo," Solomon snapped. "Hold the fort, Shane. OK?"

Before Shane could say anything, Solomon was gone. "Too bad if it wasn't," he muttered and kept firing.

The Delta commander dropped beside Turbo and the first thing he noted was that the operator was bleeding from at least two wounds. One low down and the other higher up in the right side of his chest. "You good?" he asked.

The Delta man sent out a burst of fire before he answered. When he did his voice sounded tired. "Not really, Boss. I feel pretty fucked up, actually."

"Hang in there, buddy, we'll have you out of here soon."

"Yeah," Turbo replied skeptically. He lifted his head to fire at a running ISWA soldier and a bullet punched into his head.

"Fuck!" Solomon cursed and fired at the shooter. The terrorist was flung back with a couple of bullets in his chest. Three more seemed to take his place, and for the first time Solomon thought that they may be in far greater trouble than he figured. He pressed the talk button on his comms and said, "Fall back and close the perimeter."

He fired another couple of shots and made to fall back. The bullet that clipped him along the side of the head didn't kill him, but it sure turned out the lights.


"What happened to Solomon?" Fritz asked Shane.

"I don't know," Shane replied glancing about their perimeter. It was then that he noticed Solomon was not the only one missing; there was no sign of Turbo, or the three Nigerians. He turned to Truck. "Where is Solomon?"

"I don't know, man. I ain't seen him."

"Are you OK?" he asked the Delta man indicating blood on his arm and leg.

"I'll fucking live."

Shane turned around and faced forward. He raised his weapon and fired at another terrorist. The man swiftly dropped behind cover and then rose up and fired his AK in response. 7.62 rounds fizzed through the air close to where the DEA was taking cover. A cry of pain drew Shane's attention and he turned to see his partner down and bleeding.

"Christ, no," he blurted out and hurried to Fritz's side. The man had a wound low down to the right of his navel.

Shane put pressure on the wound to stanch the bleeding, but his efforts were futile as the cherry-red liquid continued to ooze between his fingers and refused to stop.

"I told you this was a bad idea," Fritz gasped.

"Hang in there, Paul. We'll get you out of here soon."

"Yeah, right."

Shane took his hand and said, "Here, keep up the pressure."

Fritz winced with the pain of his wound that had begun to radiate out from its core. His

face had already taken on a deathly pallor, and
Shane knew that the man was dying.

With a grim expression on his face Shane
turned away and went back to the fight.

Fritz lasted barely ten minutes, leaving this
mortal world while the rest of his group were
fighting for their lives. One hour after his
death, the guns fell silent altogether.

### Ovarro City, Mexico

While the last vestiges of battle died away in
Borno State, Nigeria, the convoy in Mexico was
rolling out early in the morning. Both teams of
operators were inside armored Humvees with
machine gunners sitting in the turrets of the
first and last vehicles. Once through the gates,
they turned left and headed out of Ovarro toward the town of Cardoso.

Kane and Cara rode in the lead Humvee
with Cruz. Thurston, who would normally
stay behind in ops, was in the second one with
Ojeda. Today the general wanted to see up
close what had happened so she could get a feel
for the situation. Behind them came Arenas,
Brick, Axe, and his friend, Fredricks. Bringing
up the rear were two more Humvees containing Cruz's men.

"What do you know about these Scorpions,

Carlos?" Brick asked Arenas.

"They are said to be the best of the best," he told the ex-SEAL. "When I was commanding my special forces, I lost some of my men to them. They were always recruiting the best from all of the units."

"To get stronger?" Brick asked.

"No. Because they were always getting killed. I lost one man to them and two days later he was dead. Along with five others. They have a high mortality rate."

"They didn't try to take you, amigo?" Axe asked.

"Yes, but my wife, she was most upset, so I stayed where I was. Besides, life was dangerous enough already."

They rolled along the streets toward the outskirts of the city. They passed a line of stores with painted marks all over them and Fredricks asked, "What does all that mean?"

"The writing on the stores?" Arenas asked.

"Yes."

"It is the cartel's way of telling people that the stores are protected by them."

"Why?"

"Because they do it for the money. The owners have to pay the cartel every month the price that they ask for, and in return no one tries to steal from them because to do so would be to steal from the cartel."

"What happens if they refuse?"

"Then the cartel kills them, and they replace them with whoever they want to run the store."

"Hey, we're slowing down," Brick said as they approached an overpass. "Lock and load."

Axe turned to Fredricks and gave him his 416. He smiled at the confused Justice man and said, "Hold this and don't shoot me in the ass." Then he climbed to his feet and out of the turret where a .50 caliber Browning M2 awaited.

Axe racked the slide and chambered the heavy caliber round into the breech. Then he swept left and right looking for anything suspicious. A third of the way through his second sweep he paused and looked up at the side of the overpass. Hanging from a rope tied around its feet looking stark white against the cold gray of the concrete was a headless corpse.

The ex-recon marine spit over the side of the Humvee as though trying to eradicate a foul taste in his mouth. Over the noise of the wind blowing past the armored shield in front of him, he heard Fredricks ask something of Brick but couldn't make out what the reply was.

His gaze drifted back to the headless corpse and the sign painted in red paint beside it. As they got closer, the single word became evident. It said, Traidor.

So, the dead man had been a traitor. Now he was an example.

Beneath the overpass were three parked police cars. Six officers stood there looking up as though trying to work out how to get the corpse down.

The convoy passed by and Axe climbed back down into the Humvee. He took his 416 from Fredricks and noticed that the man was pale. "Don't let it get to you, Mister Fredricks. Things like this are commonplace south of the border."

"It's fucking ghastly," the Justice man cursed, making Axe smile. "What are you grinning at?"

"I just never thought I'd hear something like that come out of your mouth."

"I'm not a boy scout, you know!" Fredricks snapped.

"No, sir, I guess you aren't."

In the Humvee ahead of theirs, Thurston and Ojeda were also in conversation. "I don't know how you do it," Thurston said to her. "I've been in battles, led men in combat, but seeing shit like that day in and day out would get to me after a while."

Ojeda nodded. "You learn to tune it out after a while. Somehow become immune to it."

"Why did you join the Mexican Intelligence Service?" the general asked.

"The reason you saw back there," she replied. "One of those corpses hanging from the overpass years ago was my husband. He was a lawyer who refused to bow to the cartel."

"I'm sorry," Thurston said, kicking herself for asking. "Did they get who was responsible?"

She shook her head. "No. But maybe one day we will."

They traveled in silence after that. The convoy cleared the city and drove the sixty kilometers to Cardoso. What they saw upon their arrival resembled something out of a holocaust movie.

# CHAPTER 6

*Cardoso, Mexico*

Kane looked out the window at what was left of the town. The charred, blackened remains looked like a landscape from some of the war zones he'd been in over the years.

Cara said, "These people didn't stand a chance."

"There were one-hundred and forty dead," Cruz told her.

"That's terrible."

"It is only getting worse," Cruz explained. "The theft of petroleum fuel is almost a daily occurrence in Mexico. It is a wonder that more incidents like this do not happen."

"And Amaya Caro is the one behind it all?"

Cruz's voice hardened. "Amaya Caro is it all. "In the beginning, there were a few of them doing it. But once she came onto the scene she took over. Anyone who did not comply with her wishes, disappeared."

The convoy stopped and everyone disembarked. Kane had his 416 locked and loaded while he scanned his immediate surrounds. The Scorpions dispersed into a perimeter around the vehicles, while the rest of Team Reaper looked around. Kane pressed the transmit button on his comms and said, "Bravo Four, copy?"

"Good copy, Reaper One."

"Anything pop up on ISR?"

"Can't see anything with the satellite, Reaper, but we're picking up some radio chatter that we'll keep monitoring."

"Roger that, let me know if anything changes."

"Is there a problem, Mister Kane?" Ojeda asked him curiously.

"No, ma'am. Just a bit of radio chatter."

She shifted her gaze to Cruz who nodded and called to one of his men. The soldier hurried across and the Scorpion leader, said something and the man hurried away to one of their Humvees. "Now I'll ask if there is something wrong?" Thurston said.

Ojeda gave a slight shrug of her shoulders. "It may be nothing, but we've found that radio chatter always increases before an attack."

"We came across that in Afghanistan," Kane said. Then he used his radio, "All callsigns be on your toes. Chatter has gone up and we could be in for visitors."

"Can you show us where the line was tapped?" Thurston asked Ojeda.

They walked toward the edge of the village to where the damage was worst. Whole buildings had been flattened into masses of blackened rubble. Even the earth was scorched black. Except for the thirty-foot square patch of freshly-turned earth.

"This is where it was," Ojeda explained. "The company has fixed the pipe and buried it again. Sadly though, there will likely be another tap here within a couple of days."

"That quick, huh?" Thurston asked.

"It is like the little boy trying to plug the dike. We are fighting a losing battle."

"I guess that's where we come in?"

"Yes, I guess it is."

"Reaper One, copy?"

"Good copy, Zero."

Thurston glanced at Kane and waited for the transmission to continue. "We might be onto something. Approximately five clicks to your southwest looks to be a trucking yard. From the looks of it there are four fuel tankers inside."

"It could be just that, Zero."

"I thought so too at first, but ISR has at least eight guards patrolling the fence line. All armed."

"Roger, Zero. Wait one," Kane said and turned to Ojeda. "Is it commonplace for trucking companies to have armed guards walking the perimeter?"

She frowned. "Not really. Why?"

"Zero, send through the coordinates and we'll go and check it out."

"Copy, Reaper. They're on their way."

"What is it?" the intelligence officer asked.

It was Thurston who answered. "We think we might have found a transit point for the fuel."

### Five Kilometers, Southwest

Kane passed the binoculars across to Cruz and asked, "What do you make of this?"

He studied the trucking yard from the ridge where they lay, and grunted, "They are cartel."

"You think those trailers are full of fuel?"

"Most probably."

"Then we need to do this without causing a firefight."

"Yes. I think that would be best."

Kane thought for a moment. "Do you have a sniper on your team?"

"Yes, his name is Pedro."

"Good. Get him up here."

On the ridge, Thurston and Ojeda quietly joined Kane and Cruz on the ground, not interrupting the pair while looking out over the trucking company compound. But now, the general was curious. "What have you got in mind, Reaper?"

"With two snipers up here on the ridge we can take out two of the guards with ease. I intend to take a small team down there and take out the rest. Once we've secured the compound, then I guess the rest is up to Flavia."

Ojeda nodded. "You secure the compound and I'll call for some trucks to get the stuff out of here."

Kane looked back to Thurston. "Ma'am?"

"OK. Do it."

Kane toggled his mic, "Cara, Brick, Axe, on me."

From the base of the slope behind them the three Team Reaper personnel began the steady climb towards the crest. Once they were all present, Cruz and his sniper included, Kane laid out his plan for them. "Cara, you and Pedro set up overwatch here and wait for my command. Brick and Axe, you're with me. We'll use the brush as cover and get close enough to take out the other guards. Cara the two guards at the front gates are yours and Pedro's."

"Copy that."

"Right, let's go."

"Wait," Cruz said. "I will go with you."

Kane hesitated. The last thing he wanted to do was tell Cruz that because he didn't know him, he only wanted to use his own men for the op. So, instead he replied, "You get the important job, my new friend. If we get into any trouble, I need you to save our asses. If we're all committed and the shit hits the fan, we'll be screwed."

Cruz smiled but his eyes told a different story. "Like the US cavalry, yes?"

Shit. Kane pulled him aside. "All right, some of what I just said is pure horse shit. The truth is, I don't know you or your men. Until I do…"

Cruz said, "I would probably do the same thing, my new friend. But if this is to work, we will have to start trusting each other at some stage."

"You're right," Kane acknowledged and turned to Brick. "You stay here."

"Roger."

"Cruz, do you have a suppressor for that thing?" Kane asked indicating the FX-05 Xiuhcoatl assault rifle.

"No."

"Brick trade weapons with the captain."

Without question, Brick swapped his 416 for the FX-05. It should be good to go, Captain."

"Thank you."

"Hey, Brick," Axe said to the big ex-SEAL. "Keep an eye on Fredricks for me."

"Can I shoot him?" Brick asked jokingly.

Axe gave him a broad grin. "Don't do that, you'll piss mama off."

The three of them slipped over the crest of the ridge and through the brush, circling to their right to have a clear approach to the front gates. The guards were armed with AKs, a solid reliable choice, but where cartels were concerned, they had a tendency to acquire a mixed bag of weapons from across the globe thanks to the arms trade.

There was a patch of low ground that ran almost parallel to the fence line and was also screened by brush. It looked as though it had once been an old watercourse and had smoothed stones scattered in the bottom of it.

After traversing it, they came out at the point they needed to be, with Kane in the lead. Cruz was behind him and Axe pulled rear security. They stopped amid some brush fifteen meters from the chained gates. The two guards stood inside the compound, chatting. Kane said in a low voice. "Whenever you're ready, Reaper Two."

Two heartbeats after getting confirmation the two guards jerked and fell to the dusty ground. "Let's go," Kane ordered and the three of them came clear of the foliage, weapons shouldered and moving swiftly toward the gates.

Upon reaching the double steel mesh barricade, Kane fired a shot into the lock and it came apart. "Made in China," he said to no one in particular, before pushing the right-side gate open. "Talk to me, Bravo Four."

"You've got a tango at your one o'clock behind the office building."

Kane dropped his sights onto the corner of the building and tracked it as he pushed forward. Behind him Cruz and Axe swept left and right.

As he cleared the corner of the building, a sentry with an AK appeared. He caught the movement and his face filled with alarm. Bringing his weapon around to fire, he was too late and was belted hard by two blows to his chest.

Behind him, the Team Reaper commander heard the flat slap of a suppressed carbine, followed by the shatter of glass. "You get him?" he asked without turning.

"Roger," came Axe's reply.

They pressed on further into the compound. Kane emerged from behind a tanker trailer and found two more cartel guards. They cried out in alarm and swung their weapons up to meet the threat. The 416 fired again and the first man fell, his finger squeezing the trigger on his AK reflexively as he went down. The spray of bullets from the weapon cut through the hot Mexican air, lucky to miss anything explosive. The second guard fell beside the first thanks to Cruz remained unflinching despite the plethora of lead being slung around. That still left two more in the yard; somewhere.

"Talk to me, Slick. Where are they?" Kane asked.

"You've got two more—"

The rattle of automatic gunfire cut off his last words as the remaining shooters appeared from behind the tanker trailer at the far end of the compound. Geysers of dust made a beeline towards Kane as the bullets tracked directly for him. He dove to his left and he almost felt the rush of their passing. Behind him, Cruz and Axe followed suit to clear the firing line. "Fuck me!" Axe blurted out. "Shoot that fucker!"

From the ridge overlooking the compound, Cara watched the unfolding events and knew they were in trouble. Taking a deep breath, she sighted on the first shooter with her CSASS and squeezed the trigger. Seeing the falling body through her weapon's sights, she shifted her aim to cover the second shooter and repeated her actions. The second cartel man dropped like a stone, and she said, "Two tangos down, Reaper One. You're clear."

The three of them climbed to their feet and Kane looked toward the ridge line. "Thanks, Reaper Two."

"She is good that woman," Cruz allowed.

"Fucking-A she is," Axe growled. "She's saved our asses more than once."

Kane said, "Bravo, copy?"

"Read you Lima Charlie, Reaper One."

"Compound is secure."

"Roger that. We'll be down shortly. Out."

Five minutes later the convoy arrived at the compound. Cruz set his men up as security while the rest of them looked around for anything of use. Ojeda seemed impressed by the work they had done but knew that this was just the tip of the iceberg. She also knew that the cartel would plan reprisals for what had happened.

Cruz was talking to Kane when his second in command approached and pulled him aside. After a brief conversation, the man walked off. Cruz turned back to the Team Reaper commander and said, "There is still a lot of chatter that our intelligence is picking up. It all indicates an attack somewhere."

Kane frowned and scanned the surrounding landscape but came up with nothing. "Bravo Four, are you still picking up the chatter from before?"

"Roger that, Reaper. It sounds like they're preparing for an attack, but unless they're underground it's not at your position. ISR has absolute zero. So, whatever their target is, it isn't there."

Kane lost himself to thought for a moment. Just like Afghanistan the increase of ICOM chatter signified an attack. He'd bet his left nut on it, but if it wasn't there then...

"Zero, the compound is the target. I say again the compound is the target," Kane blurted into his comms.

"Repeat your last, Reaper One," came Ferrero's reply.

"Damn it, Luis. Get everyone out of there."

"Reaper, what's going on?" Thurston called out.

"The cartel is going to hit the compound. We have to get back, now!"

**Ovarro City, Mexico**

Ferrero felt dread sweep across him when he finally realized what Kane was telling him. He threw the headset down and turned to his people. "Everyone get your weapons now. Go! Full body armor."

"What's happening Luis?" Traynor asked.

"The Durango Cartel are about to hit this compound," he said before turning to Cruz's second in command, a thin man with a thick goatee. His name was Armando Ortiz. He had once been a sergeant in the Mexican army until being headhunted by Cruz himself. "Have your men stand to, Sergeant. Warn those at the gates we're about to be attacked."

Ortiz gave an abrupt nod and turned away to talk into his comms. Ferrero walked across to a bank of screens hooked into the security cameras rigged around the compound. Each covered a certain area but there was no guarantee there weren't black spots in the perimeter.

Before the teams had rolled out, Cruz had placed ten of his men to work as overall security. But should the cartel muster a large enough force, there was always the possibility that they could overrun the compound. Although Kane had urged them to leave, Ferrero knew enough from past experience that to leave a fortified position in the middle of enemy territory, especially when you didn't know where they were, wasn't the wisest of decisions.

Bravo Team reappeared, each one dressed in tactical gear including ballistic helmets, and armed with 416s and their M17 handguns. Ferrero faced them and said, "Everyone onto the roof. We'll work in pairs, Traynor, you're with me. Slick, I want you watching all of these screens. "You're our eyes. I know it's not complete coverage but it's all we've got."

"Got it, boss," Swift replied and seemed almost relieved that he wasn't about to get shot at.

"The rest of you, get going. I'll join you in a moment."

They hurried off and the operations commander turned to the Mexican sergeant. "My men are ready, Captain," Ortiz said to Ferrero.

"I'm not a captain, Ortiz. Just call me Luis. I want two of your men on the roof with my people. Can you do that?"

He nodded. There are only two ways into the compound. I can spare them."

"Thank you."

Ferrero picked up the vest and carbine that Reynolds had brought for him There was also a radio with a headset. As he hurried toward the door, he called back over his shoulder. "I'll be on comms if you want me."

"That's good, sir, because we have incoming at the main gate. And they look like they mean business."


Pete Traynor could feel sweat trickling down the back of his neck from the heat of the Mexican sun as it kicked up from the concrete rooftop. He watched on as a single vehicle flanked by at least five shooters moved along the street toward the main gate. In the distance above the rooftops he could see black smoke rising into the sky.

"Somebody knows what they're doing," Ferrero said as he crouched down beside Traynor where he sheltered behind the thick concrete parapet that wrapped around the rooftop.

"Yes, but this is Mexico, not Yemen," Traynor replied.

"Burning shit to set up roadblocks is one way to ensure help won't reach here anytime soon," Ferrero pointed out.

Behind them two of Ortiz's men arrived. The operations commander pointed to another spot on the rooftop and said, "You two over there."

"What do you make of this, Luis?" Traynor asked.

Ferrero turned back and watched as the vehicle stopped, and the cartel soldiers riding on the running boards dropped off. With its engine roaring loudly, the beat-up SUV shot forward, gaining momentum with every second that passed.

"They're going to ram the gates!" Traynor exclaimed.

Both he and Ferrero opened fire with their 416s at the vehicular battering ram. Below them in the courtyard the Scorpions did the same. The noisy rattle of the combined gunfire echoed from the lower walls and began to rise. Bullet strikes on the vehicle were noticeable from the distance. Holes were punched into the grill, others in different quarter panels. The windows disappeared and the thing lurched to a stop.

Upon this, however, the cartel soldiers that had been escorting it opened fire with a furious barrage of lead which gouged chips of concrete from the wall Ferrero and Traynor were sheltered behind. They ducked down. More bullets cracked as they passed close overhead.

On the other side of the roof, Teller and Reynolds opened fire. "Brooke, what have you got?"

"Ten tangos trying to breach this side gate."

"Keep them out."

"We're trying."

Down below in the courtyard at the front of the school, a shout was heard and one of the Scorpions dropped to the gravel. Ferrero saw one of the man's comrades rush forward, grasp him by his collar and drag him into cover behind a Humvee. Other cartel shooters raked the semi-truck and trailer, dealing out as much damage as they could.

Outside the fence the cartel was taking casualties. The defenders' outgoing fire was taking a toll on the attackers. The escort for the battering ram had dropped from five to two. At the rear near the second gate, Reynolds and Teller had cut the number of shooters by half.

Then, as quickly as it had started, the attack petered out and the shooters disappeared. An eerie silence descended across the school and Ferrero glanced about to see where the cartel soldiers had vanished to.

"Slick, where'd they go?"

"I don't know. One minute they were there and then they were gone."

"Keep an eye out. I bet they're regrouping."

"Roger that."

"Hold the fort, Pete, I'll be back in a moment," Ferrero said, dropping out his almost empty magazine and replacing it with a fresh one.

"I got it Luis."

Keeping low, the operations commander hurried across to where the two Scorpions were stationed. "You men OK?"

They nodded. "Si."

From there he went across to Reynolds and Teller. "You OK?"

Reynolds turned to face him, and he noted the small cut on her right cheek. "We're good."

"What happened there?"

She wiped away the blood and said, "Bit of concrete. Nothing much."

"Your ammunition good?"

"Yes."

"All right. Keep your head down, they'll be back soon."

As he traversed the rooftop once more, Ferrero said into his comms. "Bravo this is Zero, over."

There was a moment of silence before Thurston came over the radio. "Read you Lima Charlie, Zero."

"We're in contact with cartel soldiers. They've tried to breach both gates, but we've managed to hold them back so far. One of the Scorpions is down and we've set up a defensive position."

"Copy, Zero. We're on our way back to you. ETA approximately ninety mikes."

"Be aware that the cartel has set up multiple roadblocks, so I'm thinking you might want to double that time. I estimate they've sealed off –" he looked about. "Maybe two or three blocks in all directions."

"Hang tight, Luis."

"Yes, ma'am. There isn't much more we can do. Zero out."

"Bravo out."

Ferrero rejoined Traynor and the pair settled down to wait for the next attack. Their wait wasn't long, and when it came, it was with a bang, literally. A rocket-propelled grenade screamed out of the darkness and hit the edge of the building directly below their position. Fortunately, they'd seen it coming and had managed to dive to the hard rooftop. That, however, provided no shelter from the shower of concrete chunks that rained down on them.

"Fuck me," Traynor growled as he sucked his lungs full of air. "These pricks are getting serious."

But that little show was just the precursor of more to come. Over on the other side where Reynolds and Teller were taking cover, the cartel had brought up more firepower. "Luis we've got a mortar on this side."

"A what?"

"A mortar!"

"Shit," he snapped and looked at Traynor. "Keep your head down."

The operations commander began to jog across the rooftop toward his team members, when he found out for certain that the cartel soldiers did indeed have some kind of mortar. He heard Reynolds cry out, "Incoming!" in his ear and then the world in front of him exploded.

The air whooshed from Ferrero's lungs as he crunched into the hard roof with his left hip and shoulder. Jagged, razor-sharp, slivers of steel scythed through the air above him as well as deadly hunks of concrete. He coughed and clambered to his feet. Skirting the hole in the rooftop he made it to where Reynolds and Teller had taken shelter. "Where's that fucking mortar, Broke?" he managed.

"Over at our ten o'clock."

Ferrero brought up his 416 and found a target. He sprayed the Mexicans' position and saw them scatter, taking the mortar with them. "Let's hope the bastards aren't smart enough to set it up somewhere sheltered."

His hopes were dashed only moments later when another mortar round was launched and landed in the compound below them.

"It would appear that they're smarter than we think," Teller said searching for the new threat.

"No, it's a second one."

Another round came in and landed short. The two Scorpions down below ducked behind a brick wall, as it exploded and showered them with debris. "Something's not right," Ferrero said. "Bravo Four can you see anything?"

"Negative, Zero. I can't see anything."

"Zero this is Bravo, sitrep, over."

He suddenly remembered that Thurston, even though she wasn't there onsite, was able to monitor their transmissions. "Bravo, we've now got mortars. I say again, we've got mortars shelling us."

"Good copy, Zero."

"Keep your head down, Brook."

He ran back across the rooftop and slid to a halt next to Traynor as another round came in. The ex-DEA undercover said, "As long as we stay up here, they're going to rain mortar rounds down on us. We need to get to shelter."

"Yes, I know."

"Well –"

The crunch when it came seemed to rattle the whole building. The two men looked at each other and Traynor asked, "What the fuck was that?"

He and Ferrero ran to the east side of the building and were joined there by the two Scorpions from the west side. Down below was a burning vehicle that had been driven into the fence and exploded, fully intending to breach it. Now there were at least ten cartel soldiers coming in through the opening.

"Damn it," Ferrero growled. He snarled into his comms as Traynor and the two Scorpions opened fire, "Sergeant Ortiz, get men around to the east side; we have a breach in the fence."

By the time Ortiz replied to the command his words were drowned out by Ferrero's own 416. He managed to drop four of the cartel soldiers before they disappeared in through a side door just as Ortiz and two of his men appeared, too late.

"Shit," the operations commander growled. He said into his comms, "Slick, we've got six inside the building. Watch your ass." And as he started across the roof he said, "I'm on my way."

# CHAPTER 7

*Ovarro City, Mexico*

Swift glanced around the room, looking for any form of cover. He hefted the 416 to his shoulder and covered the entrance to the room they had set up as their operations center. He felt the nerves tingling through his extremities as minutes seemed to drag into hours. Ferrero's reassuring voice came to the read-headed tech, "I'll be there shortly, Slick. Just find yourself some cover until I do."

The room in which the ops center had been set up was previously a spacious classroom, larger than a Western schoolroom, the ceiling supported by strategically placed posts made of stout concrete posts. He side-stepped across to the nearest one and waited, hoping that Ferrero would get there before the cartel men.

Not afraid to use the weapon, he just preferred not to. His thing was computers, not a hell on a holiday firefight.

Swift heard their footsteps out in the hallway. He knew it had to be the cartel men because of the sheer number of footfalls. He dropped the red dot sight onto the doorway and curled his finger around the trigger. Did he have it on auto or semi? Did it matter?

The first shooter appeared. A heavily tattooed shooter with a bandana wrapped around his head and shorts which hung down below his knees. His top was just a white singlet. His appearance could have been mistakenly taken as someone walking in off the street, not someone here to assault and kill. Close behind him was a second shooter.

Swift took a deep breath and squeezed the trigger. The 416 slammed back into his shoulder and a patch of red appeared on the first shooter's singlet. Firing again, the Mexican fell. The tech shifted his aim slightly and fired again. The shot was hasty and flew wide giving the second man a chance to shoot back.

The AK in his hands rattled and bullets sprayed wildly about the room. They hammered into the concrete post Swift was sheltering behind chewing gouges out of it, leaving behind deep pockmark scars. Others plowed into the wall while several random ones found their way to the op's equipment, which wasn't so good. "Motherfucker," Swift grumbled at the thought of his equipment being destroyed at will. He flicked the fire selector onto auto and leaned around with his 416 raised. He depressed the trigger all the way back and let loose a torrent of fire which tore through flesh and bone. "I can do that shit too, asshole!" Swift cursed at him.

The tech dropped his magazine out and retrieved a fresh one from the pouch on his chest. He slapped it home muttering to himself. "Shoot up my fucking equipment. I'll kill your ass dead, jerk."

A third shooter filled the doorway and sprayed the room with more fire. Swift ducked back when bullets fizzed past his head. "I sure could use you about now, Luis."

"I'm not far away, Slick. Hold on."

"Hold on, he says," Swift muttered firing another burst. "What else does he think I'll do?"

More bullets and concrete chips flew as the shooter pushed into the room. The computer tech felt a lead slug tear at the fabric of his shirt and knew it was only a matter of time before one of the Mexicans got lucky. He'd taken down two, but the odds were stacked against him that one of them would eventually find flesh.

Suddenly gunfire erupted out in the hallway. Shouts of alarm echoed along it and the sound of brass hitting the tiled floor resonated as well. The shooter inside the ops room whirled about to face the new threat and gave Swift all the opportunity he needed. He brought the 416 into line and fired at the distracted cartel shooter. The man cried out and pitched forward onto the hard floor, blood pumping from the multiple wounds in his torso.

"Slick, you OK?" Ferrero called out.

"Clear in here."

The ops commander entered the room and looked around. "You look like you had a time of it. You good?"

"I'm not hit."

"What about your equipment?"

He glanced at it. "Of that I can't be certain."

"Check it out and then get back to me," Ferrero ordered.

"Yes, sir."

"Pete, how are we looking up there?"

Traynor's voice came back crisp and clear. "No other movement, Luis. It looks like it was just them. Even the mortars have stopped."

"OK. Keep your eyes peeled. I'll be back in a moment. We're all secure down here."

"Roger that."

"Well, Slick, what's the damage?"

"A couple of the monitors are cactus and a motherboard. A few circuits and –"

"Can you still use any of it?"

The computer tech nodded. "Sure, I can."

"That's all I needed to know."

### Outside of Ovarro City, Mexico

The city grew out of the landscape as they got closer to it. Already Kane could see the black smoke rising from the fires like beacons against the sky. The small convoy pulled off the blacktop and eased to a stop. They climbed from the Humvees and Thurston came forward to stand next to Kane and Cara. "That doesn't look good."

Kane nodded. "We're not going to get the convoy through all of that."

"Insert on foot," Cara suggested. "It'll be dark soon and it'll be easier."

"Agreed."

"You'll still need help getting through the roadblocks," Thurston said. "We could hit one and draw them in."

Cruz said, "My men and I can do this."

"That would be great. We can use the Humvees."

"All right," said Kane. "Let's get in there and get it done."

They all climbed back aboard, each of the Scorpions pulling hoods with skulls on them down over their faces. "You guys looking to frighten them all to death?" Kane asked Cruz.

"There are two reasons we use the hoods, my friend. One is to protect our identities. Some of us have families who would be marked for death if they saw our faces."

"You didn't wear them back at the transit yard."

"That is because there weren't going to be any survivors," he replied bluntly. "And the second reason for the hoods is to let the cartel know death is coming for them."

With a roar the Humvees pulled back onto the asphalt and drove toward the war zone and, with a large amount of luck, to the relief of their beleaguered colleagues.

### *Ovarro City, Mexico*

As the sun set in the western sky, it sent out long orange and red tendrils to claw back from the inevitable. The team in the school had only just managed to stave off two more heavy attacks on their perimeter; but it had come at a cost. Three more Scorpions were down, two of them died while the third had a wound requiring urgent medical attention that wouldn't be forthcoming anytime soon.

Outside the perimeter more vehicles burned; orange flames hungrily devouring all they could within the rapidly blackening shells. Around them lay the bodies of six more cartel soldiers, casualties of the last assault.

Ferrero slid down the wall and sat with his back leaning against it, exhaling a deep breath he didn't realize he had been holding. His dirt-caked face was a mess, and a streak of drying blood showed from a nick beneath his temple that had run down his left cheek. "I'm getting too old for this shit, Pete," he sighed.

Traynor looked down at his boss and gave him a wry smile. "Slowing down in your old age, Luis?"

"Old age be fucked," Ferrero snorted. "I'm just not cut out to fight wars like this anymore."

"It's been a tough exercise, that's for sure."

He nodded and pressed the talk button on his radio. "Teller, do a quick run around and check ammunition. Start with the Scorpions on the ground. I'll have Swift bring up some more for us."

"Roger that."

He watched the master sergeant hurry across the battered rooftop and disappear. "Slick, you still alive down there?"

"Last time I checked."

"Bring us up some more ammunition."

"On my way."

Ferrero sighed again and came back up onto his knees. He took out a pair of binoculars and scanned the area beyond the perimeter. There was a lot of damage to the buildings out there, scarred by bullets. He panned left and then back right. He stopped suddenly and then came back to focus on a doorway. Standing on the stoop was a figure wearing a hood. Nothing on it, just a plain black one. "Pete, get a look at the doorway to our one o'clock."

He passed the binoculars over and Traynor brought them up to his eyes. The figure was still there. "You think that's him?"

"Who?" Ferrero asked.

"You know who. You want me to say it?"

"Tell me what you're thinking."

"The American. There, I said it," Traynor grumbled.

"It could be him," Ferrero allowed.

"Shit, let's see if we can put him down." Traynor placed the binoculars on the wall and brought up his 416. He searched for the target through his sights, but the figure was gone. "Damn it."

"You miss him?" Ferrero asked.

"Yeah."

Slowly the evening drifted into darkness and the fires which still spewed black smoke turned into orange glows. The team was restocked with ammunition and the wounded Scorpion had ultimately given in to his wounds. Ferrero took a pull from a bottle of water Swift had brought up to them and felt his stomach rumble. None of them had eaten since breakfast that morning. "Slick, you want to order us all a pizza?"

"You want anchovies on it?" the tech shot back.

Ferrero grinned and could hear other members of his team chuckling. "I want thick crust," Reynolds put in."

"No mushrooms for me," Traynor added.

"And beer," Teller joined. "Must have beer."

"I'll see what I can do."

"All right," Ferrero said to his team. "Everyone get your night vision on. Let's be ready for when they come back."

"How much longer before the rest of the team gets here, Luis?" Reynolds asked.

"Not sure. They shouldn't be too far away."

"Good, I'm tired of doing all their work for them."

Ferrero smiled. "Yes, me too."


The roadblocks were staggered, and the five operators of Team Reaper reached the first one three blocks out from the school. Kane peered around the corner of the building where they sheltered and saw three hostiles, armed with AKs, illuminated by the flames of the large fires.

He turned back to Brick and said in a low voice, "Three tangos armed with AKs. This side of the roadblock and backlit."

"Roger that."

"Bravo, this is Reaper One, over."

"Good copy, Reaper One."

"We're about to breach their perimeter."

"Roger. We'll commence out attack on your word."

"Go now, ma'am."

He waited a few moments, listening. From in the distance came the chug-chug of a fifty-caliber machine gun. It was soon joined by a second. Kane looked back at Brick. "You ready?"

He nodded and placed his left hand on Kane's shoulder. A light squeeze told the Team Reaper commander all he needed to know, and he walked around the corner of the building.

The suppressed 416s of both men came to life, their expended shell casings dropping to the asphalt at their feet with a metallic jingle. The three cartel men convulsed wildly in a bizarre death dance with each bullet strike and fell to the ground, the flicker of the fire glow illuminating their motionless bodies. Behind

Kane and Brick the rest of the team emerged into the open. They all pushed forward and secured the area while Kane and Brick checked the fallen Mexicans. The ex-SEAL found a cell phone and a radio. He tossed both to Carlos. "These might be up your alley, amigo."

"Are you making this thing racial, man?" Arenas growled.

"What? No. I just thought that since the only thing coming over the radio would be Spanish—"

"See you're making it racial."

"No, no. Kane tell him—"

"Definitely racial, Brick," he replied, winking at Arenas.

"Aw, come on, guys."

"Man, you're lucky we don't have an HR department, Brickster," Cara said, pushing past him. "They'd love you at the moment."

"What the—"

"They're yanking your dick, dude," Axe told him. "You're a sucker."

"Son of a bitch," the ex-SEAL grunted and fell in behind them.

The team hurried along the street until they reached the next intersection. Before moving out into the exposed road, Cara peered around the corner of a large brick building on the north side of the junction. She saw a three-man roadblock. But that wasn't all. Along the street further to the east was an additional manned barricade.

Cara drew back. "We've got a roadblock to the east and another just around the corner."

The gunfire from the convoy still echoed along the streets. "Bravo, be aware that the roadblocks are still standing."

When Thurston's voice came back to him, he could hear the crackle of small arms fire through her comms. "There must be a hell of a lot more than we anticipated, Reaper, because they're swarming over here."

Kane thought for a moment before saying, "Suggest you pull back, ma'am, before you get cut off."

"Copy, Reaper. Might be the best idea. Good luck."

Kane turned to his team. "All right, this is what we're going to do. We're going to blow through this damned perimeter and make haste towards the school compound. Axe, you're rear security. Cara I'll need you covering the roadblock to the east as we crossover."

Cara raised her CSASS and said, "Just say when."

"Let's do it."

They emerged out into the open area of the intersection, with Kane, Brick, Arenas, and

Axe concentrating their fire on the three men at the closest roadblock. Cara, though, had her scope on the three to the east. The CSASS was a semi-automatic weapon with a twenty-round box magazine filled with 7.62 bullets. She waited patiently for something to happen, and like most plans, theirs went out the window once the first shooter behind her hit the ground and squeezed the trigger on his AK.

The three men on the roadblock to the east spun around and looked directly towards where their friends had been. Cara's crosshairs settled on the first cartel soldier's face as she called out, "Contact right."

She depressed the trigger and the CSASS kicked back into her shoulder. The Mexican's head snapped back as her bullet punched into it. Cara shifted her aim and fired at the second shooter. She was calm and calculating, even after he squeezed off a single shot in her direction, feeling the bullet fan her face. She sensed movement beside her and the sound of a suppressed 416 reached her ears. Three shots and the third guard went down, a marionette with his strings cut.

She turned to see Axe standing beside her. He nodded at her and said, "Guess we took care of them, ma'am."

"OK," said Kane through the comms. "Let's

keep moving."

The team continued along the street until they reached where it intersected with the road that the school was on. Kane scanned in both directions, taking in the carnage along the thoroughfare. Several vehicles had burned out or were still on fire. Bodies lay in heaps where they had fallen, and there were bullet holes on almost every surface he could see.

"Zero? Reaper One. Copy?" he whispered into his comms.

"Read you Lima Charlie, Reaper One."

"We're across the street from the school and about twenty-five meters to the right of the main gate, over."

"Got you, Reaper. Keep an eye out, the cartel is everywhere."

"Roger that."

"If you care to open the gate, we'll be there directly."

"Just say the word."

Kane turned to the others. "Cara right, Brick left, Axe rear security. Carlos on point with me. Let's do it. Zero, open the gate."

They came out onto the street and moved fast toward the main gate. After taking about ten steps the area erupted in violence. Shouts of alarm, gunfire, bullets flying everywhere. Ricochets kicked up from the asphalt as the team opened up, laying down as much suppressing fire as they could. A shooter with an AK appeared in a window to their right the weapon spewed its deadly payload toward them but Cara was quick enough to shut him down. An RPG flew low overhead before any of them saw it coming. The only warning, they received was a whoosh and then it was gone.

"Fuck! Where did that come from?" Axe called out.

"Keep moving!" Kane ordered. Ahead of them the double gates opened sufficiently wide for them to fit through.

"Reaper! On the right!" Cara's cry diverted the team leader's gaze and he saw the reason for her alarm. In the doorway of a building nearby, a figure with a hood stood holding what looked to be an M4 with a grenade launcher slung underneath.

"Get down!" Kane shouted.

The weapon fired and the grenade hit short of the team. It blew chunks of asphalt into the air and rained debris down on top of the prone operators. "Keep moving!" Kane shouted as he came to his feet. He blasted half a magazine at the stoop where the hooded figure stood. Splinters were gouged from the wood surrounds and the figure lurched back to get clear of the hailstorm of bullets.

The others leaped to their feet and began sprinting toward the gate while Kane emptied his magazine at the doorway. "Loading!" he called out and started to change out the empty magazine. Axe stopped and began to rake the area where his team leader had been firing, with his own bullets.

Kane tapped him on the shoulder as he went past his friend and said, "Move."

Axe turned to follow his leader until the whole team was inside the school compound.

"Well that was fun," Cara said, panting from the exertion.

"It was that," Kane allowed. "Bravo, this is Reaper One. We've made it home. I say again, we've made it home. Over."

"Copy, Reaper. We've pulled back about a klick and waiting to see what happens next. Out."

"Brick, check to see if there are any wounded. Carlos go around the perimeter and make sure it's tight. Axe and Cara on me."

They made their way up onto the rooftop where they found the others. Ferrero looked relieved to see them. "It's good to see the reinforcements arrive, Reaper."

"They were pretty thick out there," Kane said. "Then there was a guy with a hood who tried to blow the shit out of us with a grenade launcher."

"We saw him earlier," Ferrero told him. "We figure he's The American."

"Amaya Caro's man?"

"Yes."

"Makes me wish I'd gotten the bastard," Kane snapped.

"Not to worry. At least they've stopped dropping mortars on us."

"You want me to belt him, Reaper?" Cara asked.

Ferrero frowned. "Why?"

And true to form, the first mortar fired. Kane opened his mouth and shouted, "Take cover! Incoming!"


The fighting ebbed and flowed throughout the rest of the night and by the time the first vestiges of daylight broke over the eastern horizon, the defenders were in desperate need of a rest. But the cartel seemed to be boundless, unwilling to give them respite. They threw themselves against the walls again in a concentrated attack but failed because their hearts weren't really in it. Since the first attack they'd lost around thirty men. Now as the last attack failed and died, one of Amaya's lieutenants approached Franks and said, "The men have had enough. We have lost too many and they are still dug in like ticks on a dog's ass."

The American nodded. He knew what he had to do. Even that last attack had been one too many. Amaya wasn't going to be happy, but they had given their all and had paid a heavy price. If only he had fighters like that under his command.

"Tell them to pull back. We're done here."

"Si."

Franks moved, feeling the tug of pain in his left arm where the bullet had burned a furrow through the flesh thanks to the shooter who'd sprayed bullets at him. "We will meet again, buddy. When we do, you won't be so lucky."

The convoy rolled in an hour after the cartel pulled out. The roadblocks were cleared and the Ovarro police moved in after the fact to show they had a presence. The debrief was long and tedious, especially for those who'd been on the front line since the day before. And as they finished, they fell into their cots and slept the sleep of the bone-weary.

Ferrero was the last to face Thurston and Ojeda. "They tell me you saw him," Ojeda said.

"The American?" he shrugged. "We think so. He wore a hood like in the stories they tell."

"You were lucky you never lost anyone."

Ferrero touched his cheek. "Few cuts and scrapes. The Scorpions didn't fare as well as us. How was your jaunt out into the wilds?"

She told him about the trucking transit station and the assault on it. Ferrero looked at Thurston and said, "After the way they attacked us I think maybe we should take the fight to them instead of sitting around waiting for the next attack. Let's put them on the backfoot."

The general agreed and turned to Ojeda. "Could you do us up a package of possible targets?"

The intelligence officer thought for a moment and said, "I'll get it done up. Do you want flesh and blood or material?"

"Both. Once the team has rested up, we'll get after them. Let's hit this bitch hard."

"So be it."

"Luis," Thurston said to Ferrero. "Go and get some rest. See Brick and get cleaned up first. Then sleep."

"I'll be fine, Mary. I—"

"Do it. That's an order."

He pushed himself up out of the chair and groaned.

"Are you OK?" Thurston asked.

"Not as young as I used to be. Can't roll around the battlefield like these young whippersnappers."

The general chuckled. "Get out of here."

# CHAPTER 8

*Borno State, Nigeria*

Mike Shane groaned and rolled away from another savage kick to his ribs. He could already taste the blood from his split lips inside his mouth. "Lay off, you heathen motherfucker," Ward Solomon cursed at the Nigerian terrorist and strained to get free of his chains.

"Shut up, Infidel!" the man shouted at the Delta commander. "You will be next. Maybe Abadi will make you the first example of what happens to western imperialists who do not belong."

"Go right ahead, asshole," Solomon growled. He figured he was dead anyway. But maybe he could get them to kill him quickly.

Shane coughed and felt a busted rib grate together. Another moan of pain.

There were four of them still alive. Shane, Solomon, Truck, and Grady. After they'd expended their ammunition and been overrun, they'd been taken captive. Homer had still been alive then. Albeit shot through the leg. However, the ISWA shooters had realized that carrying the wounded man was going to be more trouble than what he was worth, so they shot him in the head.

Truck had been wounded too, but his was upper arm so he could still walk. Solomon had been dragged in by two ISWA men while Shane had fought on bravely until a terrorist had knocked him cold from behind.

The last one, Grady had just lay huddled in some low ground until the shooting had stopped. None of the Nigerian soldiers had survived.

The mud hut where they were being kept was hot and stuffy. The scent of human excrement from the bucket in the corner mixed with it and became almost suffocating. Flies buzzed around it and in the African heat it would be only a matter of time before any wounds became infected or the prisoners became diseased. If they lived long enough that was.

A figure appeared in the doorway; a big man framed by the bright light of the sun at his back. "Get them outside."

Men entered the room and the prisoners were dragged to their feet. Shane, still stunned, moaned in pain. Solomon was unchained and pushed one of the ISWA terrorists away from him and moved to the DEA man's side. "Get your fucking hands off him. I'll do it."

A questioning glance brought a nod and the Nigerian stepped back. Outside, the clean air on their faces felt good. They breathed in deeply, fully aware that it could their last chance to enjoy it. Overhead the sun was bright, and they shielded their eyes until they became used to the harsh glare. It was also the first time they had an opportunity to see their surroundings in the daylight.

It looked to be a small village made of mud huts with thatched roofs. Everywhere they looked there were armed men. Solomon did a quick calculation in his head and figured to be at least a hundred ISWA fighters, possibly more.

They were all lined up before the big man who had an aura about him. Solomon studied him for a moment. He was tall, muscular. His face was almost handsome except for a thin scar that disappeared behind a thick beard. This was Abadi Falomo, the leader of ISWA.

The terrorist stared hard at each man in silence. Others gathered to watch with anticipation. His gaze stopped at Solomon who stood there trying to stare him down. Falomo nodded. "You are the leader?"

"Maybe."

"Why were you in our lands?"

"Got lost."

"You are American?"

"Australian."

Falomo gave him a knowing smile. "You lie."

"If you say so."

The terrorist studied the rest of the group once more. His gaze locked onto Grady. "Who are you?"

"I work for the World Health Organization," Grady answered.

"A doctor?" Falomo asked with a cocked eyebrow.

"I specialize in communicable diseases."

"What diseases?"

"We received reports that there was an Ebola outbreak up this way."

Falomo stared at Grady and for a moment Solomon thought he might actually buy it. Then the terrorist's face twisted into a mask of disdain. "You lie. I think you—" he paused and shrugged. "It doesn't matter why you are here."

He waved one of his men forward. In his hand he held a broad-bladed scimitar. "Is it ready?"

The man nodded. "Yes."

"Good," Falomo replied taking the shiny blade. "Pick one."

The ISWA man signaled to another and they grabbed Grady. "What are you doing?" he gasped out.

They ignored his question and dragged his struggling form away from the others. "What are you doing, asshole?" Solomon growled and lurched forward.

One of the guards moved swiftly and clubbed the Delta commander in the back of his head. He slumped to his knees, stunned.

Truck went to his aid and slammed a fist into the terrorist's face. Three more of them descended upon the Delta man and soon he joined his commander on the ground. The only one left standing, although barely, was Shane.

He blinked to focus his eyes and saw that Grady had been dragged over to what looked to be a block of wood near a glowing fire. One of the Nigerian terrorists looped a leather strap around his hand and pulled it across the block. Another man joined them to hold Grady still. Falomo walked over to them and stood close. It suddenly registered to the DEA man what was about to happen.

"Drugs," he whispered hoarsely.

Falomo turned his head. "What?"

"We were told there were drugs up here. Cocaine. We came looking for it."

"Who do you work for?"

"The DEA."

"I see." Falomo's movements were swift as his arms moved up, over, and back down. The razor-sharp blade of the scimitar cleaved through flesh and bone without slowing. The taut leather strap went slack as the hand separated from the arm just above the wrist.

Wide-eyed, Grady began to scream. He stared at the stump where his right hand had once been, blood pulsing with each heartbeat.

"No!" Shane gasped. "What have you done?"

"That is a lesson in what happens if you lie to me, white man."

The three men who'd helped with the amputation grasped Grady and dragged him towards the fire. They shoved the bloody stump into the coals which elicited another scream that turned into a garbled cry before he passed out.

The sickly-sweet smell of burnt flesh drifted across to Shane and filled his nostrils. He wanted to double over and vomit, but he managed to keep his composure. Falomo pointed at Truck and said to his men, "Bring him with us. He will do."

"What do you want us to do with this one?"

"Let them carry him back to the hut."

*Langley, Virginia*

The place was buzzing. The video had appeared thirty minutes before on the internet and Melissa Smith was already watching it for the fourth time. There was no doubt who the American was who'd had his head amputated by the sword-wielding jihadi. Hell, he was one of her own. And as for the man responsible, that was easy as well. Abadi Falomo, the leader of ISWA in Nigeria.

Melissa slammed down the laptop lid hard enough to crack the screen. "Fucking asshole!" She looked up at the two people before her. "Give me something. Anything. But do it now."

Rich Brown was a middle-aged man with graying hair and a stern disposition. He was in charge of Clandestine Operations while the younger, more attractive Jessie Gray, headed up the Intelligence department. It was her that spoke first. "The video was uploaded an hour ago from somewhere in Africa. It was bounced around off a lot of shit and it appears to have originated in Cape Town. But we all know that it wasn't shot there. Our best guess is—"

"Nigeria where they were sent," Melissa cut her off.

"Yes, ma'am."

"Is there any way of telling if Truck was the only one, or do these pricks have more?"

"We have re-tasked a bird, ma'am, but it'll be a couple of hours before we've any intel. Even then there are no guarantees. However, from the words Falomo was using in his speech, my people seem to think that there may be more to come."

"I was afraid of that," Melissa said with a nod and turned her gaze to Rich. "What about you, Rich?"

"I can task another team to go have a look around if you want, Melissa, but then we risk losing another. I suggest we wait and see what ISR turns up and then we can go to SOCOM and plead our case for a full-blown raid."

"I don't like the waiting part. It gives that son of a bitch more time to publicly murder more of our people, if he has them. In saying that, I don't want another of our teams in there either. We keep losing people and we'll all be out of a job really quick. And now I have to go before the president and tell him we don't know what the hell we're going to do."

"I'm sorry, ma'am," Jessie Gray said. "I wish there was more to tell you but there's not."

"We don't even know if they found anything," Melissa said.

Rich said, "Ma'am, if anyone can get through this, it's Ward Solomon. He's a tough son of a bitch."

"Maybe, Rich. But I'm not sure if being a tough son of a bitch will cut it this time around."

### The White House, Washington DC

There were three of them in the meeting plus the president. Besides Melissa Smith, the other two were Hank Jones and Rear-Admiral Alex Joseph, commander of NAVSPECWARCOM, or Naval Special Warfare Command.

Jack Carter was a gray-haired man in his late sixties. A straight shooter with a fiery temper to go with it. He was a man who at times spoke first and asked forgiveness later. Like the others he'd seen the video of the big American dying, several times and upon each viewing he became increasingly riled. But for the moment he needed to rein that anger in and get the whole picture. "Melissa, give it all to me. Leave nothing out."

"Don't you want to wait for the others, sir?"

"There are no others," he growled. "They can do fuck all about the situation. You three can. Now, start at the beginning."

"A few days ago, I received a call from an old DEA friend who thought he might have stumbled across something in Nigeria."

"What kind of something?" Carter interrupted.

"A contact informed him that ISWA received a shipment of cocaine but there was something odd about it. Apparently, there were white men with the ISWA people, and they wore biohazard suits."

"Why would they be wearing biohazard suits for cocaine?"

"We don't know. That was why we dispatched a team with a biological engineer to have a look. It was meant to be in and out."

"Where did you send them?" Alex Joseph asked.

Melissa turned and looked at the Rear-Admiral. He was a man in his fifties with gray hair. For his appointment with the president he wore his dress whites, something he tried to avoid whenever possible. "Baga, Nigeria."

"Jesus H Christ, Melissa. Could you have dropped them any further in the shit?"

"We have to know what is going on," she defended her decision. "ISWA could be up to anything. Even a bio-weapon."

"So, you sent your team to their deaths on a maybe?"

"We don't know that they're dead," she shot back at him. "And you know that's how the intelligence community works, Alex. On maybes. If we waited on positives all the time, then we'd be playing catchup."

He knew she was right but sending operators into a seething hotspot like that didn't sit right with him. "You should have come to me. I could have organized a larger force to go in."

"Maybe I should have but by the time it all went through channels whatever was happening would be long gone. I made a decision on what I had at the time. It may have been the wrong one, but I still made it."

Joseph sighed. "You're right. So, what now?"

They looked at Carter. "What you've said does seem rather troubling but if we want to launch an operation into Nigeria, they're going to want details and confirmation that our people are still alive. Running a small op like Melissa did is one thing. But a full-blown military operation is something else. Their president is losing popularity at the moment because of his ties to the west. A lot of his people blame that for what ISWA is doing."

"Fuck his popularity," Joseph blurted out,

then, "Sorry, sir."

"My thoughts exactly, Alex. But right now, we do it the diplomatic way."

"Yes, sir."

Carter shifted his gaze to Hank Jones. "Is there something you want to add, Hank?"

"I've not said anything, sir."

"I know, your silence is thunderous."

"There's nothing I can add, Mister President. Everything you've said makes sense."

"I'd have thought cocaine was right up the alley of that team of reprobates you employ?"

"That team of reprobates, as you put it, sir, are on an assignment in Mexico."

"That's right, how's it going?"

"Let's just say it's interesting."

Carter looked at him thoughtfully. "Wait a moment, wasn't there something in the intelligence brief about some ruckus down there. Was that them?"

"Let's just say that the Durango Cartel aren't too happy about their presence."

"Durango Cartel? Who the hell is top dog in that one? They change all the time. Cut the head off one and another appears."

"That would be, Amaya Caro, Mister President," Jones replied.

"Never heard of her."

"I have," Melissa Smith said. "She's the one

behind the upshift in all of the petroleum thefts down that way."

"That's her," Jones confirmed. "The team is working with Los Escorpiones and Mexican intelligence as a joint op."

"Fine, fine. Melissa, let me know if something changes. For the moment that is all."

# CHAPTER 9

*Ovarro City, Mexico*

Five of them sat around the table looking at the intel package which Ojeda had put together. Besides the intelligence officer there was Thurston, Ferrero, Kane, and Cruz. The top page was a list of targets, both soft and hard. From suspected transshipment points and storage places, to suspected money hides and a list of high-up personnel. One, in particular, caught Kane's attention for the fact that he was based in Ovarro.

"Tell me about Felipe Flores," Kane said looking at the intelligence officer.

"He is one of the higher lieutenants in the Durango Cartel. Not that there are many of them. He takes care of business in Durango."

"He would have been involved with the attack on the compound the other day?"

"Possibly but not essentially," Ojeda replied. "What we saw at the overpass the other day would have definitely been his work."

"Will he have good knowledge of the cartel's workings if we scoop him up?" Thurston asked.

Ojeda nodded. "If you can scoop him up."

"Why?" asked Ferrero.

Cruz chuckled. "Flores lives in one of the zona prohibida, a no-go zone as you like to call it."

"Just because it is a no-go zone doesn't mean we can't go there," Kane told him. "Have you and your people been in there before?"

"Once," Cruz told him. "I lost three men in there chasing two men who killed a police officer."

"What's the area like?" Kane asked.

"It is a poorer part of the city. A slum if that's what you want to call it. It is dangerous and the cartel blends in with everyone else. You could stand next to them and you wouldn't know."

"We'll know, all right," Kane said sounding positive.

"How?"

"They'll be the ones shooting at us."

"You are crazy to go in there with less than a battalion of men."

Kane glanced at Thurston and asked her,

"Can you get us a little bird and a Black Hawk by tomorrow afternoon?"

"A phone call should do it."

"Great," Kane said sounding pleased.

"There will be nowhere to land in there," Ojeda pointed out. "How will you get in?"

"That will be the easy part. We'll rope in onto the roof of the building if we can. If not, we'll do it onto the street."

"And get back out?"

"Cruz and his men will give us a ride."

The captain snorted and shook his head. "You are loco, my friend."

Kane gave him a wry smile. "If you can get me what I need, the team and I will work out a plan and we can have a pre-op briefing in the morning."

"I'll see that you get it, Reaper," Ferrero said.

Thurston nodded. "Looks like we have ourselves a mission."


Ferrero lived up to his word and had all the intel Kane and his team would need to formulate a workable plan. Amid the process he had included Cruz because he and his men were an integral part. The next morning when they all gathered in the ops center, Kane walked to the front of the room and started the briefing.

"OK, so when we go in, we'll go in loud and hard," Kane started. "He used his finger as a pointer for the extra-large map which he was using. He traced a circle around a building in the center and continued. "This is the target building. The Black Hawk will put Axe and me over the target and we'll fast-rope down onto the rooftop. It's only three floors and a maximum of maybe nine?" He looked at Ojeda who nodded. "OK, Nine apartments. The little bird will put Carlos and Brick onto the street. Cara will remain on board as sniper when it lifts off. Carlos and Brick will sweep up and we'll sweep down. In and out as fast as we can."

"Sounds good so far," Thurston said.

Kane continued. "Cruz and his men will wait with the Humvees here a block to the west. Once we have the HVT then we'll radio and you come pick us up."

"What's your alternate extract?" Thurston asked.

"We fight like hell until we're clear. We'll be engaged, there's no doubt about that, we're going in daylight. Let's hope they're surprised enough to make it easy for us."

Cruz said, "I have been thinking about your plan and I would like to suggest a change if I may?"

Kane stared at the captain and shrugged his

shoulders. "Go ahead."

"I think we should put a Humvee with a fifty-caliber machine gun outside the house once you go in. As a deterrent. The rest of my men will wait."

"Can't hurt," Kane agreed. "OK, we'll put a Humvee outside the apartment block. Anything else?"

"Do we actually know where this guy lives?" Axe asked.

"No."

"So, we have to sweep each apartment individually?"

"That's what we discussed."

"I still don't like that."

"It is what it is."

"I might be able to help there," Ojeda said. "Give me a couple of hours and I'll see what I can do."

Kane looked at her. "OK. We go at seventeen hundred."

"I'll have something by then."

"Slick, we'll need an eye in the sky too."

"Can do."

"No UAV, General?" Kane asked.

She shook her head. "No."

"OK, we'll do with what we have. Anything else?"

No one spoke.

"OK. Let's go. Get ready and make sure you have everything squared away."

### H-Hour, Ovarro, Mexico

The two helicopters lifted off from the airfield, banked, and pointed their noses towards the target. Aboard the MH-6S Cara sat in the front seat beside the pilot. Behind her in the bay was Brick and Arenas, both sat in the doorway with their boots rested on the running boards.

Flying off their port side was the Black Hawk carrying Kane and Axe. Once they were inserted the Black Hawk would pull out while the MH-6 would circle above the target so Cara could provide sniper support.

The helicopters flew low and fast over the city, causing the locals to look skyward as they passed overhead. The flight time would be minimal which was a good thing. Cara looked out through the cockpit bubble and could see the slum coming up off the nose. "One minute," the pilot said into the comms.

Christ, they'd only just got airborne. Across in the Black Hawk Kane and Axe would be getting the heads-up. She went through a final check of her CSASS and then made sure her safety strap was secure. With that complete she waited as their target grew larger in the distance. Before leaving, Ojeda had come through with good intel telling them that their HVT was in apartment four on the second floor.

The MH-6 came in fast along the street causing any civilian traffic there to scatter. The pilot was better than good and didn't hesitate. He flared the bird just before the skids hit the asphalt.

Brick and Arenas exited the MH-6 and dropped to a knee, sweeping the area while being buffeted by the helicopter's downdraft. The MH-6 picked itself up and started to fly a pattern overhead which would allow Cara to do her job.

"Reaper Three and Five on the ground and entering target building," Arenas radioed as he and Brick started toward the main entry door of the apartment block.

"Good copy, Reaper Three," Ferrero acknowledged.

Behind them came the roar of a Humvee engine as the vehicle accelerated down the street and screeched to a stop on the street outside the building. In the gun turret a masked Scorpion sat behind a fifty-caliber and began sweeping the immediate area. Cruz stepped from the vehicle and Arenas heard him say over the comms, "Scorpion One in position."

"Roger that."

The sudden appearance of an armed man at the front door of the apartment block caused Arenas to react and he fired his 416, knocking the would-be shooter back. "Contact!" he called out then pressed forward, disappearing inside with Brick behind him.

Kane and Axe fast-roped from the Black Hawk and touched down on the rooftop. They immediately began making their way toward the door access, their weapons raised and ready. "Reaper One and Three entering the target building."

"Good copy, Reaper One."

Behind them the helicopter departed and the whop-whop of its rotor blades quickly faded away. Kane tried the door but found it locked. He raised his right foot and kicked out. Wood splintered as the frame, weakened with dry rot, gave way and the door flew back. He was about to step into the stairwell when he heard Arenas' call of contact and was immediately on edge.

The smell of piss and other odors assailed his nostrils as the draft from the open door where Arenas had entered, wafted up the stairwell on the cross breeze and out the top like a chimney. "Someone's been pissing in the stairwell again," Axe growled.

"Could be worse," Kane replied. "You could have fallen in dog shit again."

They pushed down to the third-floor landing and Axe stopped. "You want to sweep this floor first?"

"Nope, target first. Once we hit the second-floor landing you post security outside the door."

They started to move off when the door was flung open and a shooter appeared, armed with an AK-47. "Hey, putas," he shouted.

Axe's 416 rattled briefly, spewing brass casings from its ejector, which bounced down the concrete stairs. The cartel man spasmed and fell to the floor, three bullet holes in his chest. "Stupid fucker," Axe growled and left his muzzle centered on the open door should there be more to follow. When none appeared, he followed Kane down the stairs to the second floor. Arenas and Brick were waiting for them when they arrived.

"You ready?" Kane asked.

"Let's do it."

Beyond the door they could hear raised voices. Kane touched the doorknob and turned it. No sooner had he begun to pull when the door splintered outward, wicked slivers of wood scything through the air. They all recoiled as more bullets punched through the thin door. Kane waited for the moment that the shooter was reloading, then pulled the shattered door open.

It swung back and Brick stepped into the void, his carbine spouting fire, cutting down the shooter in the hallway who dropped dead. More appeared from doorways, filling the narrow hall with deadly fire. Brick dropped the first couple of Cartel soldiers and pushed further inside. Behind him came Arenas and then Kane. On point Brick took down another shooter who spilled from a doorway, with two bullets in his chest.

When they reached the apartment they required, the door was open and a dead cartel soldier lay over the threshold his blood staining the carpet.

Brick peered around the doorjamb and was greeted by a spray of automatic weapon fire from a MAC-10. Holes were stitched across the wall opposite the doorway and forced the ex-SEAL to pull back. He reached up to his webbing and pulled a flashbang free.

The pin came free and Brick tossed the stun grenade through the opening. The flashbang detonated and he entered the apartment.

The apartment contained three men. Two were armed with MAC-10s while the third held only a handgun. All three, however, were dazed and shaken from the flashbang. Brick hesitated for only a moment while he took in the features of all three. Recognizing the man he wanted, he shot the other two then pressed forward and dropped Flores with a sweep of his right leg. The cartel lieutenant cried out as he fell to the floor and Brick moved in swiftly and rolled him onto his stomach. While he tugged the cable ties tight, Kane and Arenas finished clearing the rest of the apartment.

Brick pressed his talk button and said, "Jackpot, I say again, jackpot. We have the HVT in custody and are coming out."

Kane looked down at Brick and said, "Let's go."

They pulled Flores to his feet and pushed him towards the door. A few minutes and they would be on their way out. But then the chug-chug noise made by the fifty reached up from the street below. The radio burst to life and then an explosion blew out the apartment windows. It was followed by a cry of, "Contact! Contact!" and the neighborhood erupted in a roaring great gunfight.

"Where the hell did they come from?" Cara exclaimed watching the streets below her fill with cartel shooters. The track from the RPG which hung lazily in the air was starting to dissipate. She tracked it back to its origin and got the perpetrator in the CSASSs sights. She squeezed the trigger and the man fell, the launcher spilling to the street.

"Reaper One, copy?"

"Copy, Two."

"The streets are sprouting tangos, Reaper. You need to leave now."

"We'll be out in two mikes."

"If I was you, I'd make it less."

The MH-6 banked and came around, the fact that an RPG had been used made the pilot nervous and unwilling to stay put. Cara said into the boom mic, "Bring me back in from the north."

"Copy, ma'am."

The little bird swooped around and gave Cara a better picture of the streets below. The alleyways behind the buildings were teeming with cartel shooters that streamed towards the target building. She saw the Humvee convoy pull up out front behind Cruz's vehicle. There were now five lined up ready for the extraction.

"Be aware, Reaper, you're walking into a shit storm out front."

"Copy."

That was when the first Humvee blew sky high.

"Fuck!" Cara snapped, staring at the contrail from the second RPG. "Zero, did you see that?"

"Roger, Reaper Two."

Then to the pilot, "Get me in closer to that building to the northwest."

"Yes, ma'am," the pilot answered and brought the MH-6 around so she could have a clear line of sight to the structure where the RPG had come from.

On the ground the Humvees were now engaged in a full-blown firefight. Cara could see at a glance the Scorpions sheltering behind the armored vehicles, returning the incoming fire.

She raised the CSASS to her shoulder and said to the pilot. "Hold here, Heath."

"That'll make us a stationary target, ma'am," Heath the pilot protested.

"Exactly, do it."

The MH-6 came to a hover and almost immediately bullets plinked from its exterior. "We can't stay here, ma'am, we're a frigging bullet magnet."

"Just wait a moment," Cara snapped keeping her sights focused on the window of the building from which the RPG had been fired.

More bullet strikes.

"Ma'am."

"Wait."

Still the shooter didn't appear.

"Damn it, ma'am, we can't stay here. I'm coming out."

"Wait, damn it! If we don't get them the team is screwed."

Then the shooter appeared ready to fire once more. Cara shot first and he fell back from the window and disappeared. "Go, now."

"Coming out!" Heath barked and before he'd finished the two-word sentence the MH-6 was lifting up and away.

Suddenly the MH-6 began to vibrate almost uncontrollably. Heath the pilot cursed out loud and Cara asked, "What's up?"

"We're going down."

"Shit," she cursed. "Zero, Hawkeye One is going down, I say again we're going down."

"Copy, Hawkeye. Good luck."

# CHAPTER 10

*Avarro City, Mexico*

Kane looked skyward as soon as he heard the call and saw the MH-6 starting to drop off to the northeast. He cursed under his breath and said into his comms, "Bravo Four, get a location on the crash site as soon as they touch down and send me the coordinates. We'll move there once we have them."

"Roger, Reaper One. Will do."

"Reaper One, this is Zero."

"Read you Lima Charlie, Zero," Kane answered as more bullets slammed into the Humvee he was sheltered behind.

"Reaper, we understand your concern. but you still have a package and wounded to extract, am I right?"

"Cruz can do that. We will make our way to

the crash site on foot, secure the area and wait for extract."

Thurston came on the comms. "Reaper, Bravo, over."

"Send, Bravo."

"That's a negative on the request. We've no way of knowing when we'll be able to get you out."

"That's not a request, Bravo. We're going."

"Damn it, Reaper—"

"Reaper One out."

Beside him Axe nodded in satisfaction. "We all go home, Reaper."

"Oorah," Kane shot back.

"Amen to that."

Bullets kept peppering the Humvees and the intense fire was met by the booming sounds of the fifty-calibers. Kane kept low and sent his next transmission to Cruz. "Scorpion One, Reaper One, over."

"Copy, Reaper One."

"Listen up. Get your men and wounded into the Humvees. My team is going to stay and go to the crash site. Take the HVT with you. Once you get back to the school, take care of things and then come back for us."

"You take a mighty big risk, my friend."

"I'm not leaving until I know the situation of those on board the helicopter."

Things became personal for Kane at that moment. They weren't just "those" on the helicopter. One of them had been with him from the start. Cara was family and there was no way he was going to leave her out there. The Team Reaper commander turned to Axe and said, "Get Flores over to Cruz and then come back."

"Copy that," Axe said, grabbing the cartel man by the arm and dragging him away.

Kane glanced over the hood of the Humvee and saw an insurmountable number of cartel soldiers shooting in their direction. He picked out a Mexican who broke cover to shift position, and killed him with a couple of shots.

"Reaper, I have a location on the helo," Swift said to him. "It is around five blocks to your northwest."

"Any sign of survivors, Slick?"

"Negative."

Kane fought back his emotions and said, "Reaper Two, copy?"

Silence.

"Reaper Two, this is Reaper One. Do you copy?"

More silence.

"Come on, Cara, cowboy up."

"Give me a minute to find my hat," her voice came across sounding pained.

A smile split Kane's lips. "That's my girl. Sitrep, Reaper Two."

"We fucking crashed."

His smile broadened. "Come on, Cara, adapt and overcome."

There was another long silence and he imagined her looking around trying to get her bearings.

"We're down, the chopper is in one piece. Heath is out to it but alive."

"What about you?" Kane asked.

"I hurt but I'm ambulatory."

"OK, fort up. We're coming to you. Just hang in there."

"Copy. Hurry up, people are starting to gather."

"Is your weapon operational?"

"Affirmative."

"You do whatever you have to do to stay alive. Reaper out."

"Reaper One to Zero."

"Good copy, One."

"Luis, dispatch Bravo One, Two, and Three to the crash site just in case we can't get there."

"I'm on it, Reaper."

"Thanks, Luis. Reaper out."


Ferrero turned to Traynor who was watching things unfold on the big screen with Reynolds and Teller. "Gear up, get a Humvee and get your asses out to the crash site."

There was no hesitation in their response as they turned and hurried off to the equipment storage. Traynor grabbed himself a vest and a 416. He then found a ballistic helmet and attached some grenades to his webbing.

Next to him, Reynolds and Teller did the same, except Reynolds grabbed a weapon with a grenade launcher beneath the main weapon. She looked at Traynor and said, "Time for payback with these assholes."

"You're right," Traynor said and put the 416 back to pick up a SAW. "Let's give it to these fuckers."

They returned to the ops room and found Thurston waiting with Ferrero. She said, "Be careful out there; you don't know what you're driving into."

"We'll be fine, ma'am," Reynolds reassured her.

"If you can't get through, pull back and we'll think of something else."

"Yes, General."

Thurston watched them go and said to Ferrero, "I hope we didn't just bury more of our people, Luis."

"The way the screen's lighting up, Mary, it might be more than just those three."

"Maybe we should order Reaper and his people out."

"You know as well as I do, that is one order Kane would refuse to follow. I think the best we can do right now is give them some air support."

Thurston agreed and turned to Swift. "Slick, reach out to our Black Hawk. Get them over the crash site. They're weapons-free if need be."

"Yes, ma'am."

The General picked up a headset and said into the boom mic, "Reaper Two, this is Bravo, over."

"Read you Lima Charlie, ma'am."

"We're going to divert the Black Hawk back to you. Hang in there, help is coming."

"I'm not going anywhere, ma'am."

"Slick, has the helo turned?"

"Yes, General. ETA approximately ten mikes."

"Ten mikes? Why so long?"

"I don't know."

Thurston glared at him. "I'll find out."

"You do that."

She studied the screen which was now concentrated over the crash site in a three-block radius. Thurston frowned and then pointed at the left of the screen and asked, "What are those there?"

No one answered her and it irritated her more. She turned to Swift and snapped, "What the fuck is going on down in that fucking corner?"

Swift punched in a few keys and the satellite zoomed in. For a moment they stood there and watched before realization took over. "Fuck me," Thurston said, shocked at what she was seeing. "Tell Reaper to pull his ass into gear before they overrun the crash site. Now, damn it!"


"Reaper there's a group of cartel bastards running parallel to us in the alley over to our left." Brick called out from behind his team leader.

"We need to pick up the pace then," Kane called back over his shoulder as they double-timed along the street. Up ahead, Arenas ran point while Axe pulled rear security.

A burst of gunfire was followed by, "They're pushing up behind us."

"Keep moving," Kane barked. "We have to get to that crash site before the cartel overruns it."

Except for a few vehicles, the street seemed to be deserted which made the Team Reaper leader both relieved and nervous. Relieved because he couldn't see them, but nervous because no visual didn't mean they weren't there. They could be laying in wait to ambush them. "Bravo Four, how far out are we from the crash site?"

"About a block and a half, Reaper One."

"And the cartel?"

"They have some boots at the site now, but the main force isn't far away."

"Bravo One?"

"Two mikes."

"What about the Black Hawk?"

An ominous silence was heard over the comms.

"Slick? The Black Hawk?"

"We don't know, Reaper," the tech replied. "It took some fire and they had to put it down to check it out."

"Shit. Let me know when it's back up."

"Roger that. Out."

From the rear of the mobile column, Axe called out, "Our friends have ducked off to the left. I think they've tagged onto the crowd that's running parallel."

"They're making the crash site their priority."

"Then you better run faster."

A bullet ricocheted off the side of the broken helicopter a foot or so above Cara's head. The shooter exposed himself long enough for her to get a bead on him and punch his ticket with a bullet to his face. The cartel soldiers were steadily building, and it wouldn't be long before they would have enough men at the crash site to surround it and keep Reaper and the others out.

From inside the downed MH-6 she heard Heath moan. He'd been doing it for the past few minutes and she decided he was hurt worse than she first thought. Cara, however, had been lucky. Her back was a little tight and there was a small cut on her forehead, but other than that she was fine.

A bullet snapped close to her head. Almost fine.

To her front, Cara saw three cartel men start to push across to her right, trying to flank her. The CSASS slammed back against her shoulder and the first runner went down in a tangle of arms and legs. She shifted her aim and dropped the second. Shifted her aim once more and squeezed the trigger.

Nothing happened.

"Shit," she swore and rolled to her left. She changed out the spent magazine for a fresh one and rolled back. But by then the third Mexican was gone.

More bullets fizzed through the air. Cara found the shooter and sent him to hell along with the others she'd dispatched so far.

From her comms Cara heard, "Reaper Two, check fire. Reaper One, Three, Four, and Five are coming in from your south. How copy?"

Cara looked to her south and saw Kane standing sheltered on a street corner. "Good copy, Reaper One. I've got you. Be aware it's getting mighty sporty around here."

"Roger, Two. We're inbound."

The team broke cover and ran towards the downed helicopter. They dropped in behind the minimal amount of cover that was provided and started to mount a stern defense of their position. "Brick, check out Heath."

"On it."

"How are you doing, Cara?" Kane asked, giving her a quick once over.

"I hurt but other than that I'm fine. I'm glad to see you guys though."

"There's a heap of cartel shooters coming this way, so we need to get out of here. Once Brick's finished, we'll move."

The roar of an engine sounded from the street behind them and an armed Humvee appeared. Standing in the gun turret manning a fifty caliber was Traynor. The vehicle came to a stop and Reynolds and Teller dismounted.

The chug-chug of the heavy caliber machine gun filled the street. It blew big chunks out of not only the buildings, but cartel shooters as well.

"Brick, how's Heath doing?"

"He's got a busted leg and is a little banged up. Otherwise he's fine."

"Then give him some Morphine and Phenergan and we'll get him the hell out of there."

"Done on both counts, Reaper."

"Carlos, give Brick a hand to get him out."

"On it."

It took several minutes for them to extricate Heath from the wreckage and lay him on his back beside the MH-6. "I'm going to insert an IV cannula before we move him any further, Reaper," Brick said above the gunfire.

"Hurry it up before these fuckers get around us."

"Too late," Reynolds called out as a fusillade of bullets blasted in from the opposite direction. She slipped a grenade into the launcher slung beneath her weapon and let it go. An orange explosion rocked the area where it detonated, and shouts of pain rang out.

She opened the launcher once more and slipped another in. This time she did a one-eighty and lobbed it into the area from which the most concentrated fire was emanating. "Reaper," Axe called out. "That's a woman after my own heart right there."

"If you've got your grenade then now would be a good time to use it," Kane told him.

With a nod Axe produced his small package and pulled the pin. He threw it and called, "Frag out!"

When it blew, he was rewarded with cries of pain. Suddenly the Black Hawk appeared overhead. "Reaper One this is Joker One, copy?"

"Read you Lima Charlie, Joker One."

"We heard you might need some help. Sorry we're late, some asshole tried to shoot us down with a BB gun."

"Better late than never, Joker One. We could use a pass from east to west on the south side of the street, over. Danger close."

"Roger that. East to west, danger close. Mark your position for us, Reaper One."

"Give me a minute, Joker."

Kane looked about but saw nothing useful. Axe, I suppose you don't have a smoke marker on you?"

"Sorry, Reaper. Left it at home beside my bed."

"Thought so."

Across the street a red vehicle caught his eye. "Traynor, hit the red car across the street."

The ex-DEA undercover shifted his aim and pumped shot after shot into the vehicle until it exploded into flames.

"Joker One we've popped smoke."

"I must say it's novel, Reaper One. I see black smoke. I repeat, I see black smoke."

"The black smoke marks the enemy position, Joker. Anything north of that, regard as friendly."

Even though it wasn't entirely true, it would reduce the possibility of a friendly fire incident. The Black Hawk pilot came back over the comms. "Roger that, Reaper One. Hang onto your panties, Joker One inbound."

The Black Hawk came in low and hard, the door gunner working the minigun. The rounds cut through the air like a hot knife carving through butter. It wreaked untold devastation upon the cartel soldiers and was even worse when they turned and came back. All of a sudden, it didn't resemble a Mexican city anymore. It looked more like the pictures on television portraying Aleppo, or some other hot war zone.

"Let's go while they've got their heads down," Kane said. "Axe, Carlos, with me. Brick you ride the Humvee with the others and keep an eye on Heath and Cara."

"How are you getting out if you don't come

with us?"

"Leave that up to me," he said with a wry smile. Then he said into his comms, "Bravo, cancel the Humvee extract from the Scorpions. The area is too hot."

"Understood, Reaper One."

"Joker One, copy?"

"Yeah, read you Lima Charlie, Reaper One."

"You see that three-floor building behind us?"

"Roger that."

"Meet us on the rooftop for extract."

"That ain't going to hold the weight of this bird, Reaper One."

"Then don't touch down, we'll be there in three mikes. Out."

The Humvee roared away along the street with Traynor still playing hell with the fifty-caliber. Once they were gone the rest of the team headed inside the building that had been designated for their extract, and started up the stairwell.

Upon reaching the rooftop they came under immediate fire from the one across the street. Axe and Arenas hunkered down behind the small brick wall and began to return fire while Kane called in the Black Hawk. "Be aware Joker One the LZ is hot, over."

"Just be ready to haul your asses onto this

thing, Reaper One," the pilot shot back. "No time to fuck around."

One minute later the Black Hawk came in to hover half a foot above the rooftop. The door gunner had the minigun firing flat out while the three operators climbed aboard. Then only seconds after the last man climbed in, the pilot took the helicopter up and out of the fire zone.

Kane looked over at Axe who smiled at him, pumped up on adrenaline. "Man, that was some hot shit down there, Reaper."

Kane nodded.

"What else could go wrong?"

Kane's expression changed as he reached for his M17.

"Now just hang on a moment, Reaper. Don't go doing anything silly. Reaper? Reaper…"

### Mexico City, Mexico

Franks hung up the cell and stared across at Amaya. "How many?" she asked, her voice chilled.

"Twenty, maybe more."

"Dead?"

"Yes."

She let out a string of words that would have made a marine blush, before she turned back to Franks and asked, "How many did they lose?"

"None. Just a helicopter."

"Why did they come into the slum?"

"You know the answer to that already."

Amaya nodded. "They were after Felipe."

"Yes."

"Fucking putas," she barked.

"Does he know much about the shipment from Africa?"

"A little. But he doesn't know when or where. Only its origin."

"Should we change the port of entry?"

Amaya thought for a moment and agreed with the suggestion. "Yes, do it. Also, I want no more fighting with the Americans until after the two shipments have arrived from Africa."

"But the second one is not for another month."

"And the first one will be here within the week," Amaya snarled. "Just do as I say. My reputation is at stake and I want nothing to damage it. Understood?"

"I will organize for the shipment to be changed and put the word around that the Americans are to be left alone."

"Thank you."

"Is there anything else?"

"No, get out and leave me alone."

# CHAPTER 11

*Langley, Virginia*

Rich Brown and Jessie Gray were back in Melissa Smith's office and once again the news was all bad. ISWA had posted another video, this time it was of Ben Grady meeting the same fate as had the Delta man Truck.

"This shit has got to fucking stop," Melissa growled. "What do we have?"

"Not much, ma'am," Jessie told her boss. "The only thing we think we know is that they may have moved."

"May have or have?"

"We're not sure."

"Damn it to hell we need to get another team in there, and the president is sitting on his hands."

Rich Brown said, "I can't get a team in there

unless we go dark, and if that goes sideways, we're all screwed."

"There might be one other way," Melissa said grimly.

"What's that?" asked Brown.

Melissa picked up her desk phone and said, "Get me Hank Jones."

General Hank Jones was in Melissa Smith's office an hour later, sitting in a chair opposite. "Do I need to guess why I'm here, Melissa? Not that I need to, it's a no-brainer."

"I need your help, Hank."

"I guess you do," he said casually. "Or is it my team you need?"

"They are the only ones at the moment who have a chance in hell of getting those people out and finding what the hell is going on."

"They're in the middle of an operation, Melissa," Jones pointed out.

"Pull them, Hank. You and I both know this is more important."

"You want me to send my people into one of the most dangerous places on this earth at the moment to save your ass, am I right?"

"If it makes you feel better to say it that way, then, yes. The president won't authorize an assault, and I sure as shit can't send a black ops team in there. That leaves your team to go into Nigeria looking for a shitload of cocaine and two missing DEA agents. From where I sit, they're about the only damned people that can do it."

"No."

"What? Hank –"

"I said no, Melissa. I'm not pulling my team from one death trap and putting them into another one that is by far worse. We almost fucking lost them yesterday. As it is it cost us an MH-6."

Melissa was about to plead some more when his cell rang. He put up his hand to stop her and then answered. "Jones."

He listened for a while and then nodded a couple of times. Grunted once and said, "Hold on, Mary, I'll put you on speaker. I'm with the Director of the CIA, Melissa Smith." He placed the cell on the oak desk, pressed a button and said, "Say that again, Mary, so we can all hear it."

"I said that our man here has given us some intel about a shipment of cocaine coming out of Africa."

Jones looked directly at Melissa and said, "That is why I'm going to send my team to Nigeria."

### *Ovarro City, Mexico*

Once the team arrived back, they rested for a while and let Flores stew before Ferrero and Traynor went in to interrogate him.

They sat across from the thin-faced Mexican who had a goatee beard and a single gold tooth, and waited, staring at him. After a minute, Ferrero said, "Have you enjoyed your stay?"

Flores looked at him as though he were stupid and said, "What the fuck you on about, American pig?"

"I'm just asking if you've enjoyed your stay? That's all."

"What the fuck do you think?"

"Hey," said Traynor. "No need for the disrespect. He's just trying to be nice."

"Are you assholes stupid or something?"

"No," said Traynor. "But you are."

"I what?"

"You're stupid. You got caught. Now what we're going to do is ask you just once to help us out. If you don't, we're going to hand you over to the Mexican police. Who knows, you might even end up dangling from an overpass like the ones the other day."

"Fuck you."

Traynor's hand moved like lightning. His

right fist grabbed a handful of Flores' hair and dragged his head forward and down. There was a sickening crunch as the cartel lieutenant's face impacted the stainless-steel table and flattened his nose. Flores reeled back with blood pouring from the battered appendage.

"Talk, asshole, or we'll put you in a hole so fucking deep you'll never see daylight again," Ferrero growled.

"You broke my nose, man," Flores cried out.

"Here, give me a look at it," Traynor said. He tilted the Mexican's head back so he could get a proper look at the busted nose. Then he reached out and twisted it. "I can fix that."

A howl of pain echoed throughout the small room and it was quickly followed by, "All right! All right, I'll tell you whatever, man. Just let my nose go."

Then Flores spilled everything he knew including the drip of information about a shipment of cocaine coming in from Africa.

"I just got off a call from General Jones," Thurston explained to everyone in the room. "We're going to be re-tasked to Africa."

"What's going on, ma'am?" Kane asked.

"A whole lot," Thurston said and then began to elaborate. "A while back, a couple of DEA agents in Nigeria got wind of a cocaine shipment which was linked to ISWA."

"Is this something to do with our bird in the cage?" Cara asked.

Thurston nodded. "It could well be."

"What would ISWA be doing with cocaine?"

"I'll get to that," Thurston explained. "The DEA informant told them about the cocaine, and also of white men in biohazard suits. Mike Shane, the DEA agent on the ground with his partner Paul Fritz, requested help from the CIA who dispatched a Delta team led by Ward Solomon."

"Ward is a good guy," Brick said. "Good operator."

"Something went wrong. They got caught by ISWA and now they're in a world of pain."

Now everyone in the room was alert. "How much pain?" Kane asked. Since being in Mexico they'd not really seen any news reports.

"What we know for sure is that ISWA executed two of them and posted it on the internet," Thurston explained.

"Who?" demanded Brick.

"A Delta operator known as Truck, I'm not sure of his real name, and a biohazard specialist named Ben Grady."

"Fuck it," growled Axe.

"Because there is cocaine involved, we've

been asked to go and have a look."

"I thought you said we were re-tasked, ma'am?" Cara queried.

The general nodded. "That's right, but I figure you people have the privilege to refuse. This is not a normal op. You're going to be going into one of the most dangerous places on the planet."

"Why not hit them with a full assault?" Kane asked.

"Too complicated to explain. But it's us or nobody. The objective will be the drugs. If we find the prisoners while we're conducting the operation, then so be it. However, there is a good chance that where we find the drugs, we will find our people."

"I'm fucking in," Axe stated. "Let's go kill these assholes."

"Me too," Brick stated.

"Just hold on," Kane said. "We may operate as a democracy, but when it comes down to it, I have final say on ops like these."

"We have to go, Reaper," Brick said. "There's no two ways about it."

Kane ignored him and stared at Thurston and Ferrero. "What about our op here?"

"We'll come back to it at a later point. But they could well be linked," Ferrero answered.

"What are we taking, support wise?"

Thurston said, "You tell me."

"LSVs?"

"No. You'll drop in."

"An Avenger?"

"No."

"I'll need a Raven in case something happens. Extra ammo, grenades, and grenade launchers."

"We can do that."

"What about Bravo?"

"What about it?"

"Where are you going to be based?" Kane asked.

"Djibouti. USAFRICOM. Camp Lemonnier."

That gave them pause for thought. Camp Lemonnier was around four thousand kilometers away from their area of operations. Thurston continued. "This is a recon mission. You'll be out on a limb, miles from home. You get caught you're screwed, plain and simple. There is no coming back."

"I want an extra body."

"I'll see what I can do."

"I have a question," Axe said.

Thurston nodded in his direction. "Ask it."

"How the fuck are we meant to get back if we get the prisoners?"

It was what they were all asking themselves,

but Axe was the one who gave voice to it.

"There will be a CH-47 on standby to pick you up when you need it."

Axe frowned. "I thought you said—"

"I know what I said. Even when you radio for it, the bird will take at least an hour to reach you."

"Where's it coming from, Brooklyn?"

"Just know that it'll be there when you require it."

"What's the target area?" Kane asked.

"Baga."

"Damn it, I can't believe that they were allowed to go in there in the first place."

"They were, they did, and they are. I need an answer. There's a lot to do before we go."

There was nothing to like about the mission at all. They were to drop in the middle of a furnace with not much of anything including support. Kane ran his gaze over his team, this could well get them all killed. "Talk to me."

"I'm in," Axe reaffirmed his position.

"Me too," Brick said.

Cara nodded. "I'll go."

Kane stared at Arenas and saw the uncertainty in the Mexican's eyes. He had the most to lose of anyone. A wife and kids. "It's OK to say no, Carlos."

"I am not scared of dying, John," he said using Kane's first name. "My family—"

Thurston said, "If you go, Carlos, and something should happen, I promise that they will be looked after for as long as they need it."

Satisfied with her response he said, "I will go."

"Let's get prepped. I'll see if I can get you an extra body for the mission. You have anyone in mind?"

"Normally I'd say we take Traynor, but for this op I want a hardened operator. Someone who knows Nigeria and ISWA better than we do."

"Tell me who he is, and I'll get him."

### Mogadishu, Somalia

"Bulldog One, your target should be in the café opposite your current location."

Knocker Jensen stopped his pedaling of the bike and dropped both of his feet to the dirty street. He turned his head so his brown eyes could assess the small building opposite with the pale blue paint peeling from its bullet-pocked walls. Standing either side of the doorway were two, armed, dark-skinned, militiamen carrying AK-47s. "Fucking bollocks," he cursed as he took his aviator sunglasses off. "Are we sure the fucker is in there, Nightingale?"

"Roger, Bulldog. The tracker that was put on his clothing has him in there as we speak."

Raymond "Knocker" Jensen was a hardened SAS veteran from 22 Squadron for fifteen years, most of it spent fighting in the war on terror. He'd served in Afghanistan, Iraq, Yemen, Syria, Egypt, and a dozen other countries across the globe where he'd killed more terrorists, fought more battles, and lost more men than he cared to remember. Now his current assignment had him working for MI6. He figured that eventually it would get him killed. But after Syria he didn't care. But if he got the opportunity to take some terrorist assholes with him when it happened, then even fucking better. Especially this terrorist asshole.

He was a solid-built man in his mid-thirties. He had dark hair and a dark beard. Underneath the flaps of his coat, tucked in his belt on both sides were two Browning nine-millimeter handguns with spare magazines in the inside pockets.

"Do you have any idea of how many bodyguards this fuckhead has?"

The man he referred to was Hassan Ali Muse. An arms trafficker who supplied the Somali warlords with more hardware than they would ever need. This was the closest they'd been to him since MI6 had missed him in Switzerland twelve months before.

"No idea, Bulldog. Could be two, could be twenty."

"Great, so I could die before I even get fucking near him," Knocker growled.

"Good luck, old chap."

"Fuck you."

Knocker parked the bike and walked across the street towards the café. The two guards stepped across to block his path. "No," the one on the left snapped.

"I want to get a cup of tea," Knocker said.

"No."

"Come on, pal, just a small one and I'll be on my way."

"Fuck off, white guy," the guard cursed.

"I do wish you hadn't have said that, you cock," Knocker said and drew his left side Browning.

The guard's eyes widened with shock just before the SAS man shot him in the face. The bullet killed him on the spot and before he'd hit the ground, Knocker shot the man's partner twice in the chest.

Filling his opposite hand with the second handgun, Knocker stepped in through the doorway. The interior was dimly lit from the lack of windows. People had already started to scramble for cover while some grabbed for weapons. One of them, a tall man dressed in pants and a shirt swung a handgun up to point at the SAS man. Jensen was too old a hand to be taken by someone as slow as this prick was. Two more shots rang out from the weapon in his right hand while the Browning in his left also bucked. Two more of Muse's men went down and Jensen hadn't even made it four feet inside yet.

Shouts of alarm filled the room as another man appeared with an AK. He started to shoot wildly and only succeeded in killing an innocent patron. Knocker shot him too. In the guts, then in the head.

From the left of the room yet another shooter sprayed bullets in the SAS man's direction. Knocker ducked behind a wood pole that held up the roof. It was only about a foot in diameter, but it offered some protection.

Knocker paused there for a moment before he shot this man too. Twice in the chest so that bright red blossoms appeared on his shirt.

How many more of these pricks are there? His eyes searched the room and he saw no sign of the target. Knocker marched toward the opening which led out into the back room. He found a single table there with three more men. One was Muse, the arms dealer. Well dressed in a suit that only a wealthy man could afford.

The others were just two upright corpses who only figured it out when the SAS man shot them dead.

With the right-hand Browning centered on Muse and the left side one down at his thigh, Knocker said, "You're a fucking hard man to catch up to."

Muse wore a white suit, stained by the constant travel through the dry wasteland that was Somalia in drought. He placed a thick cigar in the ashtray on the scarred tabletop and asked, "What now?"

"Who betrayed me and my men?" Knocker snapped.

"Bulldog, what the fuck are you doing?" the voice in the SAS man's ear asked frantically.

"Come on, asshole, who betrayed me and my men in Syria?"

"I don't know what you are talking about," Muse replied.

Knocker shot him. Not in the head or chest, but in his right arm just above the elbow. Muse cried out in pain and sweat broke out on his forehead.

"I'll ask again. Who betrayed me and my men in Syria?"

"For Christ sakes, Bulldog, kill him and get out of there," came the voice in his ear again.

"Muse, answer the question."

"You are crazy!" the arms dealer screeched.

Knocker shot him again. "Who?"

More cries of pain, this time higher pitched when the bullet shattered the ball and socket joint in his shoulder. "Last chance, Muse. Next one goes into your guts and you die slowly."

"All right! I will tell you. It was Taggart. Will Taggart."

For a moment Knocker considered shooting him again for lying, but there was something in his face which told the SAS man he wasn't. "Will Taggart, MI5 Will Taggart?"

"No, he works for MI6."

Knocker shot him in the face. He turned on his heel and started toward the front room and the main exit. As he walked, he said into his comms, "I'm coming for you, Taggart. You hear me, you cock? I'm fucking coming for you."

**HMS Queen Elizabeth, Gulf of Aden**

Knocker was virtually off the Merlin helicopter before its wheels even touched the deck of the steaming carrier. He walked purposefully toward the island where the bridge was and where he knew he could find Taggart. The man he was going to kill.

The MI6 officer had been in charge of the hunt for Muse over the past couple of years.

Only he'd kept getting away, slipping the net. Switzerland, they were close. Syria, they thought they had been close but in fact, at the time Knocker and his men had walked into the ambush, Muse was on a private jet getting as far away as possible. They had been betrayed and now Knocker knew by whom. He'd lost all his team that day. He was the only one to make it out.

He was met on the flight deck by a couple of SBS guys stationed on the Queen, before he could get anywhere near the island. They'd been ordered to intercept the SAS man to prevent him getting anywhere near the traitorous MI6 agent.

"You have to stop right here, Knocker," Spud Ellis said to him.

"The fuck I do, Spud. Get out of my way."

"He's been taken into custody, Knocker. He'll get what's coming to him."

"My oath he will," Knocker said. "A nine-millimeter hollow point right in his fucking brain."

"That's what he deserves right enough," the second SBS man agreed. "But punishment isn't up to us. The head shed want to pump him for intel."

"I'm coming through, Mick," Knocker warned him.

With a sigh, the SBS operator named Mick could see the determination on his face. He stepped aside for Knocker to walk past.

He pushed his way past and as he did, Mick looped his arm around Knocker's throat and started to put him to sleep. "The SAS man began struggling but Mick had a good hold. "Don't fight it, Knocker. Let it go."

A short time later, Mike lay Knocker on the deck and looked up at Spud. "He's going to be pissed when he wakes up."

Spud nodded. "Yeah, he is."

And he was. They locked Knocker in his cabin until he'd cooled down enough for the captain to come and see him. A tall man, Captain Bill Roberts had been on the ocean for half of his forty years.

"You calmed down yet, Sergeant?" he asked formally.

"About as calm as I'm going to be while that asshole breathes, Captain."

"Yes, well, you're going to have to let it go. He'll get justice."

"I'll not hold my breath, sir. He'll not get the justice he deserves."

"Yes, he will. But that's not for you to worry about. We've had a request for your services."

"Mine, sir?"

"That's what I said didn't I?" Roberts growled. "You're to be flown to Djibouti. US-AFRICOM."

"Do you know why, Captain?"

"No. Just that you were requested by a General Mary Thurston. You know her?"

"No, sir."

"Anyway, you've got five hours to get cleaned up and have your kit sorted before your flight leaves. I'm not going to have any trouble from you am I, Sergeant?"

"No sir."

Roberts' expression grew stern. "I'd better not or I'll get those SBS blokes to toss you over the side."

"Yes, sir."

# CHAPTER 12

*Camp Lemonnier, Djibouti*

"If I'd have known you were mixed up in this, you cock, I'd have told the head shed to fuck off," Knocker said as soon as he laid eyes on Kane.

"Is that any way to greet an old friend, Knocker?" Kane asked the SAS man.

"Never said we were friends, Reaper."

"Now I'm heartbroken."

"Are you still dicking around with that big bloke? Hatchet or whatever the fuck his name is?"

"Axe, and the answer is yes."

Knocker shifted his gaze and saluted Thurston. "Sorry, ma'am. It's been a while since we've seen each other."

"So, it would seem," Thurston said with a

nod.

"General Thurston, this is Ray Jensen. Knocker."

"Pleased to meet you, General," Knocker said more formally.

"You too, Sergeant," Thurston said. She looked up at the sky through her sunglasses. "How about we get out of this damned heat and we can have a bit more of a chat?"

"Sounds good to me."

They jumped into a Humvee and took it over to the mess area. Once they hopped out Thurston grabbed one of her loadout chiefs from the C-17 and told him to take Knocker's kit over to where the team was going to be bunking.

They went inside the mess area and grabbed a couple of beers. Cara was already there waiting for them and Kane introduced him to her.

"You the one from the Philippines?" Knocker asked.

Cara looked at him curiously. "Why do you ask?"

"Reaper told me about a time in country when he and some female lieutenant held off half a terrorist army until help arrived." He stopped and smiled at her. "Least that was the way he told it."

Cara smiled at the SAS man. "That was me."

"She's the team sniper, and my second in command," Kane told him.

"Second in command of what?" Knocker asked.

Kane glanced at Thurston who said, "How about I fill you in, Sergeant?"

"That would be grand, General."

Thurston informed of the team's history and what they did and when she finished, Knocker asked, "Why am I here then, ma'am? You sound like a mighty competent team."

"Reaper asked for you. We need your help for a mission, and he tells me you're the one person he wants along."

Knocker eyed him suspiciously. "Did he, now? You make this sound kind of dangerous. Where exactly are we meant to be going?"

"Baga, Nigeria."

The SAS man chuckled. "Now I know you're having a laugh. That place is fucking red hot."

"And you know the place better than any of us, Knocker," Kane said. "You spent a week in there under ISWA's nose and they never even knew your team was there."

"Things are different now, Reaper. That cock Falomo had them organized pretty well then, but now he's got them better prepared. "Why do you want to go in there so bad?"

Kane filled him in.

"Fucking hell, mate, tick them off. They're screwed, well and truly."

Kane shook his head. "We're going with or without you, Knocker."

Thurston stood up. "We can put you on the next plane to the Queen."

"Hold up, ma'am," Knocker said. "I didn't say I wasn't going, just that it was a crazy idea."

"You'll go then?" Cara asked.

"I'll go. But have your shit in order before we do, because ain't none of us coming back from this lark."

"I can't believe I agreed to this fucking one-way trip, Reaper," Knocker said as he loaded his spare magazines for his HK 416.

"It'll be fun, Knocker. What else would you be doing?"

Knocker thought of something straight away and then pushed it out of his mind. This was going to be a mission where he needed his head straight at all times. He'd gone over all the intel with the team and from it gathered what he required. The bonus of having him along was that he already knew where the ISWA camp was. "Will your pilots be able to drop us on target?"

"They're good, Knocker. Stop worrying."

"I wish I had my normal battle carbine," he said going over his 416 again.

"There's nothing wrong with that one, Knocker," Cara assured him. "I check them all myself."

"Sorry. I just get a little edgy before I deploy."

"Don't we all?"

"You had much to do with Falomo?" Axe asked as he organized the SAW.

"Only come up against him once. Our intel before we went in was that he was the son of a pirate who was taken out by your forces back in the day. His family too. Lost them all at the one time. Grew up hard, joined the Nigerian army, and left after four years. Just long enough to get what he needed out of it. Including some specialized training from a group of SAS advisors. Once he took over ISWA in Nigeria things really stepped up."

"What was your op in the area for, anyway?" Cara asked.

Knocker stopped what he was doing, and his gaze became distant. "We were deployed to rescue a British doctor who got kidnapped from a mission in the area. They shouldn't have been there in the first place. We had a location and we dropped in at night. There were five of us. Enough to get in unseen but not enough to stand off a concerted attack if it developed.

Anyway, we laid up for five days just observing the camp to get solid intel that the doctor was there. That came on day six when they took the doctor from the hut where they were keeping him."

"What happened?" Kane asked.

"They shot him in front of us before we could react."

"Did you hit them?" Axe asked.

Knocker shook his head. "No. Like I said, there wasn't enough for a concerted battle. We, as you Yanks would say it, rode off into the sunset."

"Shit," Axe said aloud.

"Yeah. Shit."

"Gear up," Thurston called to them as she put her head through the doorway. "Wheels up in thirty minutes."

Knocker looked at Kane. "What fancy call-sign are you tagging me with? Hotdog? Rocky? Donut? Yankee Bravo English Dipshit or something special like that?"

"I like Donut," Cara said with a grin.

"You ask me," Axe commented. "I like Dip-shit."

They all chuckled, and Kane shook his head. "Nothing that elaborate I'm afraid, Knocker. You'll be Reaper Six."

The SAS man put his body armor on and

then picked up his ballistic helmet. He attached his NVGs and checked them. He had an M17, his 416 was suppressed, and lastly, he fixed his comms. He turned to Kane and said, "How do I look?"

"Like a toff."

"The lovely lady at the palace would be proud."

"I met her," Kane said suddenly.

"You what?"

"Uh, huh. Cara and I, a while back. We were wrapping something up in London."

Knocker looked at him thoughtfully and then it came to him. "The nukes? That was you? It was all kept hush-hush, but things have a way of getting out. Except for who was involved."

"Yes, that was us."

"Good fucking show, chum," he said with a nod of satisfaction. "I may not like the monarchy much, but that old girl, she's something special. It'll be a sad day when she leaves us."

"Look at you. Under all that armor you're just—"

Knocker's head snapped around to look at Cara. "You breathe a word of it, and I'll deny everything."

They all chuckled as they grabbed up their gear and started for the door.

### Borno State, Nigeria

"Everyone, check in," Kane said over his comms.

"Two OK."

"Three OK."

"Four OK."

"Five OK."

"My balls hurt."

"Glad to see you're still alive, Reaper Six," Kane said.

"Only fucking just; that branch near killed me," the SAS man groaned.

"Zero, this is Reaper One. Team is all down and accounted for."

"Good copy, Reaper One."

Through the NVGs he wore, Kane could see his team starting to come to him. Their parachutes were hastily hidden and now they were making ready to hump toward their target. With any luck they should be in position just before dawn broke.

"Knocker, you're on point," Kane told the Brit. "You good with that? Your manliness good with that?"

"Take more than getting hammered in my balls to have me skive off."

"Great. No more than a twenty-meter gap

back to the number two at all times. I don't want to go losing you and have this all turn to shit. Move out."

By Kane's watch it was eleven twenty-five. If everything went well, they should be in position by oh-three-thirty.

They pushed through the night, taking a break every hour to keep fresh, and at oh-three-ten, Knocker called a halt to their progress. The ground they had traversed was dry and the vegetation sparse. "What's up?" Kane asked.

Knocker pointed to their front. "You see it?"

"What?"

"Take your NVGs off and it might be easier."

Kane lifted them and waited for his eyes to adjust. "What am I looking at?"

"At our twelve o'clock."

Kane blinked a couple of times and then focused his eyes. It wasn't much, but it was there. A small pinprick of orange light. "Yes, I see it now."

"That's Baga. Now, if we switch course to our ten, we should make our layup position by around dawn."

"We're running that late?" Kane asked, alarm in his voice.

"Yeah, shit happens."

"Fuck. Lead on."

It took another hour to reach where they wanted to be and by that time the sun was coming up over the horizon. The team was tired and looking forward to a rest. Their OP was a small rock and brush-covered knoll about one klick from the ISWA camp.

Kane and Knocker took first watch and were in position between some large rocks when they suddenly realized something. There was no movement from the camp. That and no sign of any fires which the terrorists would cook with or use for warmth against the cool nights.

"Something isn't right," the SAS man said.

"I agree," Kane acknowledged. "They're not there. They've gone."

"The question is where?"

"Shit," Kane cursed and pressed the transmit button on his comms. "Bravo, copy?"

"Reaper One, this is Bravo One, read you Lima Charlie."

"We have a situation here, Bravo One. The local terrorists have left the building, over."

"Are you sure?"

"As sure as I'll ever be."

"Wait one, Reaper. I'll just wake them up."

"Negative, Bravo One. We'll go down and have a look and work out a plan from there. I'll call in once a decision has been made."

"Roger that. Bravo One, out."

"Let's wake them up, Knocker," Kane said to the SAS man.

"They're going to love you, mate."

"Yeah, right."

They roused the rest of the team and after a few grumbles, they were back on their feet and ready to march some more. They crossed the open expanse to the ISWA camp in relatively good time. The camp itself was a scattering of mud huts with thatched roofs. Slowly they began to clear them one at a time until they were finished.

Axe appeared with a grim expression on his face. "You'd best take a look at this, Reaper," he said.

Both Kane and Cara followed him to behind one of the rearmost huts where they found three mounds. Freshly dug. The Team Reaper commander stared at them for a moment before he said, "They murdered two, but there's three graves."

"Yeah," said Axe. "I counted that too."

"See if you can find something to scrape some of the dirt away," Kane told his friend.

"What are you going to do, Reaper?" Cara asked.

"We need to find out who that third person is. Have the others see if they can find anything that will point to where they went. Set yourself up somewhere and I want a three-sixty-degree lookout just in case they decide to come back."

"Copy that," Cara said, not wanting to be around for the grisly task.

"Bravo One, copy?"

"Go, Reaper One," Reynolds replied.

"Is Zero or Bravo on hand? Over."

"Wait one, Reaper."

Axe reappeared with a busted piece of plank. "You want me to start?"

Kane nodded. "Respectfully, Axe."

"You got it."

"Reaper One? Zero."

"Copy, Zero. The terrorists have left, and we have three fresh graves. Depending on what we find they'll need to be extracted, over."

"I'll organize that this end. You said, what you find?"

"Affirmative. We're going to try and get an ID on whoever is there."

"Roger, standing by."

It took the best part of an hour to ID the bodies. Two were the men who'd already been executed. The third they didn't recognize. It was obvious he'd been dead longer than the other two but only by a few days. "Zero, we have two PIDs and one unknown. Will send you a pic."

"Roger, Reaper. We'll run it and see what

we can come up with. Any sign of the drugs or other prisoners?"

"Negative. We'll push over to Baga and look around."

"Be careful, Reaper. We should be extracting you."

"Can't finish a mission if you aren't there, Luis. Reaper out."

Kane gathered his team about him. "What do we have?"

"Not much," Brick said. "We found where they were keeping the prisoners, but we don't know if there were any others."

Kane nodded. "OK. We're headed over to Baga."

"Not a good idea, Reaper," Knocker cautioned. "There could be ISWA crawling all over the place. Before you know it, they'll have you by the bollocks ringing them like bells."

"It's the only way we'll find out where Falomo went. We need to find the drugs and see whether there are any other survivors from the previous team."

Knocker gave an abrupt nod. "OK, then. How about you let me and someone else goes in there for a butcher's hook?"

"A what?" asked Axe.

"A look, mate. Come on, keep up."

"I knew that," Axe lied and then said, "I'll go

with him. I won't understand shit he says but I can watch his six."

"We'll need to go in without all this kit," the SAS man continued. "They'll be a bit nervous if we go in there looking like we're about to fight a war. Just take our handguns."

"Fine," said Kane in agreement. "The rest of us will wait outside of town. But you take your comms. If you get into any trouble, we'll come pull your "bollocks" out of the fire."

"You're a fucking gentleman, Reaper. No doubt about you."

They humped toward the town, but before they could reach it, things changed. The terrain was too flat and there was nowhere for them to lay up. So, they pushed on until they hit the outskirts.

"This looks fucked," Axe said aloud. He was looking at half-destroyed mud structures blackened by fire. Piles of debris and twisted corrugated iron lay scattered around. Holes blasted by bullets and RPGs could be seen everywhere they looked, and this was just the outskirts.

"What happened here?" Kane wondered.

It was Knocker who filled him in. "The Nigerian army used to have a base here. They and Boko Haram, whom we now know as ISWA, have had a few brawls over the years. In twenty-fifteen there were an estimated two-thousand deaths here alone. Then in twenty-eighteen they came back again. Supposedly only killed about ten people that time 'round but they took over the town."

A grim expression settled on Kane's face. "Listen up, we're all going in."

Knocker turned to protest but Kane cut him short. "No exceptions. Knocker, you lead us out. Axe, you watch our six. Call out anything that's hinky."

"What the fuck is hinky?" the SAS man asked.

"Not right."

"Oh, dodgy."

"Yeah, dodgy."

They marched along the middle of the streets towards the center of town. Each time they stopped to talk to someone they seemed to magically disappear. Their surroundings varied somewhat as they continued. Some areas seemed untouched by the fighting from previous years, while others wore the battle scars of small pockets of resistance.

Every so often they would pass a blackened shell of a vehicle, burned beyond recognition and left as a bizarre reminder of what had occurred here.

Suddenly to their left, three men came

charging from the mouth of a narrow alley between two buildings. Each of them was armed with AK-47s. They started to shout at the intruders as they came on, their weapon up to their shoulders but not yet pointed at any of the team. That wasn't the way it worked out for the other side. All six, including Kane himself had their weapons trained on targets, fingers on triggers waiting for any reason to put the three men down.

There were cries of, "Put them down! Put the weapons down!" amongst the jabbering of the Nigerians more than likely saying the same thing, but with all of the noise it was hard to tell.

"What are they saying?" Kane called out to Knocker.

"The same shit we are."

"Tell them we're friends."

Knocker shouted over the top of the din and Kane motioned to his people to lower their weapons. The Nigerians looked confused for a moment before they did the same. All the while Knocker kept trying to calm the situation. Before long, it was just two of them talking.

"They want to know who we are and what we want?" the SAS man told Kane.

"Tell him."

Knocker spoke to the man in his language,

informing him of their identities and their quest. The man threw his arms around, pointing in two or three directions and then talked some more. "What's he saying, Knocker?" Kane asked.

"He said that cock Falomo and his people took off yesterday. They were in trucks and headed towards Niger."

"Ask them if they had any prisoners."

After Knocker had finished, the man nodded and then spoke some more. "They had two."

"Ask him if anyone saw a white man working with Falomo?"

Once more the SAS man relayed the question and the Nigerian nodded.

"Does he know who he was?"

The man shook his head then said, "Wait. I show you something."

Knocker jerked his head around and looked at Kane as the man hurried off. "Sodding wanker can speak English."

He returned a short time later with a magazine in his hand. He passed it to Kane, open at a page he was interested in. The Team Reaper commander looked at it and frowned. He looked up at the man and asked, "Was he here?"

"Yes. Him."

"Who is he?" Cara asked looking at the picture of the gray-haired man on it.

"It says he's Paul Botha. He's South African. Some kind of biological engineer."

"He doesn't look like our other dead guy," Axe said.

"Do you know what happened to him?"

"He left. Maybe one week past. Along with trucks."

"You said the trucks left yesterday," Kane said.

The Nigerian nodded. "Yes, and the first a week ago."

The Team Reaper commander turned away and said to Cara, "We've got problems. If what he says is true, then there could be two shipments of cocaine. Mix in the bioengineer and it's not good. The question is, where to from here?"

"Prisoners first," Cara said. "We get them, and they can give us firsthand intel. We may even catch Falomo."

"Or they're already dead and we lose precious time before we find out what Falomo is up to."

"You know there's a good chance he's with his prisoners, don't you?" Cara asked.

"What if he's not?"

Cara shrugged. "One of the truck convoys already has a week on us. Then there is the second. We know that one of them is headed to the US. But where is the second headed for? We need to find Falomo to get the intel."

"Agreed," Kane said with a nod. Then into his comms he said, "Bravo Four, copy?"

"Copy, Reaper One."

"I need you to track a convoy of trucks that left here yesterday and are headed to Niger."

"I'll try but our coverage in the area is screwy at best."

"Just do what you can. Also, I need all you can dig up on Paul Botha. He's a South African biological scientist."

"On it."

"We need some wheels," Cara said.

"Knocker, ask him if there are any wheels around we can borrow?"

"What for? Wait, don't answer that. Anyway, ask him yourself, he speaks English."

After a glower from Cara, the SAS man asked his question and the Nigerian shook his head. "He says no, Reaper."

"Tell him you'll give him a hundred dollars."

"That's just brilliant, that is," Knocker growled. "Fucking hell, use my money to buy the bloody thing."

"Do it, Knocker."

Five minutes later they were standing next to a battered VW taxi van with dents in the doors and one panel on the left blackened by fire. "Does it work?" Kane asked.

"It better flaming work, I'm forking over a hundred dollars for the bastard."

"I will drive it," Arenas said.

"Be my guest," said Kane without argument.

The Mexican climbed into the driver's seat and turned the key. True to the Nigerian's word the vehicle roared to life, blowing a cloud of blue-gray smoke from its exhaust.

Knocker passed the money over and said, "You'd better be good for this, Reaper."

"It won't matter much, remember?" Kane replied. "We aren't coming back you said."

The team climbed aboard, Brick riding shotgun while Arenas drove. Ten minutes later they roared out of town and headed toward Niger.

# CHAPTER 13

*Niger, Africa*

The small yellow van rattled along the gravel road, just about shaking everyone's teeth from their heads. The landscape had changed from brown with patches of green, to flat brown with patches of brown. The grass was dry and brittle where it existed, and dirt was prevalent. Drought had hit hard in this part of Africa. According to Swift the team was headed in the right direction. Hell, it was the only damned road to follow for the past three hours.

"How's our fuel, Carlos?" Kane asked.

"The same as it was about fifty kilometers ago," came the reply.

"It's rooted, mate," Knocker called out. "I told you."

"Stop the van, Carlos."

The Mexican slowed down and stopped in the middle of the road. From the back, Brick called out, "Great place to stop, amigo?"

"You see anything coming?"

"No."

Kane climbed from the vehicle and said, "Stretch your legs. Zero, we're taking five. Let's find something to dip the tank, Carlos."

"Roger that, Reaper One," Ferrero acknowledged. "Slick might have something for you. He's located what looks like an old village maybe thirty kilometers further on. I say old but there are signs of activity."

"Send me the feed," Kane said and turned to Cara. "Break out the laptop and antennae."

Cara rummaged around and found what she wanted while Kane and Arenas tested the tank. Once the rugged computer was up and running, she said into her comms. "What do you have for me, Zero?"

"I'm sending you a feed of a village to your northeast."

Cara punched a few keys and a picture appeared. "What am I looking for?"

This time when a voice was heard it was Swift. "Do you see the village, Reaper Two?"

A gaggle of buildings appeared. "I can."

"Down in the left corner of the picture you'll notice some trucks."

"Zoom in."

The picture on the screen changed. "OK, I have them."

Swift continued. "If you notice toward the center of the picture you can make out some figures. Six in total."

"I see them, Reaper Four, but not real clear."

"Wait one. I'll tune it up."

The zoom shifted again, and this time Cara could see all six as clear as day. Even the weapons they were holding. "They look like guards," she observed. "Where are the rest of them?"

"They all left after the plane did," Swift said.

"What plane?"

Once more the picture changed. "This one. It left yesterday."

"Do you know what was on it?" Cara asked.

"They loaded it with freight as well as four men."

"I don't suppose we know who?"

"No."

"I guess we can safely say that the cocaine was aboard."

"I'd say so," Swift agreed.

"And the rest left except for these six?"

"Yes, ma'am."

"You're sure?" Cara pressed him.

"As sure as I can be."

"So, why are they still there?"

"I can't answer that, ma'am."

"Thanks, Reaper Four."

Meanwhile Kane and Arenas found a stick long enough to dip the tank and when they withdrew it, the wet line indicated that there was only around six inches in the bottom. "Not much, let's hope it's enough," Kane said.

He then joined Cara to find out what she knew. She showed him the pictures that Swift had sent her. "They left six," she finished.

"They have to be guarding something."

"Or someone."

"Let's find out," he said. "Everyone back aboard."

"Pull off here," Kane told Areas.

The landscape around them now consisted of stunted brush and rust-colored sands interspersed with clumps of long-stemmed grass. As best he could figure, the Team Reaper commander put them about three klicks from the village. Arenas parked the van behind two larger bushes beside the dirt road and cut the engine.

Kane pressed his transmit button and said into his comms, "Zero? Reaper One. We've stopped and will approach on foot, over."

"Good copy, Reaper One. Hold position, over."

Kane looked at the others as they prepared to move. "What's the problem, Zero?"

"Wait one. There seems to be an issue with the number of tangos onsite."

Kane waited for another minute before Ferrero came back to him. "Reaper One, there are now fifteen tangos at your target. I say again, one-five, that's one-five tangos at your target. Over."

"Read you Lima Charlie, Zero. Stand by."

Kane turned to the others. "We've got extras at the target. The number has now increased to fifteen."

Knocker grinned. "Should be just about even, Mate."

"You've changed your tune," Cara observed.

"The way I see it, we go in there, kill all these cocks and then go home. Bob's your uncle."

"He what?"

"Bob's your uncle? Fanny's your aunt?"

"Nope."

Knocker sighed. "You people really have to learn some of the Queen's own English."

"Once we get close enough, we'll put the Raven up. That'll be you, Cara, I'll leave Carlos with you. When we know what's going on, the rest of us will go in, take out the tangos, and see what they're guarding. Hopefully it'll be our people. Any objections?"

No one spoke. Kane nodded. "Zero, Reaper One. We're Charlie Mike."

"Roger, Reaper One. You're continuing mission."

"Raven is airborne," Cara said as she guided the small UAV with the joystick hooked into the laptop. She tested the controls and with a satisfied nod said, "Everything seems OK."

The RQ-11 Raven was a small hand-launched UAV with a life span of around sixty to ninety minutes and had an effective operational radius of approximately ten kilometers. It was powered by an electric motor and could accomplish speeds up to almost one-hundred kilometers per hour.

"Are you getting this picture, Zero?"

"Affirmative, Reaper Two."

"Reaper One, copy?"

"Read you Lima Charlie, Reaper Two."

"Raven is up and should be over the village in a couple of mikes."

"Good copy, Reaper Two."

Cara flew the UAV with deft skill gained from hours of practice. The camera scanned the terrain below until the village came into view. The village was just a scattering of thatched-roof mud huts situated around a small crossroads. On the first pass, Cara picked out thirteen tangos. When she brought the Raven back, she still came up with the same number.

"Tell Reaper we only have thirteen. Two must be inside one of the huts," she said to Arenas who relayed the message.

"Copy that, we're moving in. Out."


Ward Solomon was almost certain Shane would die soon if the assholes who were holding them prisoner didn't kill him first. He wasn't a doctor by any means but knew a dying man when he saw one. The moans in his sleep. The cries of pain. The beating they'd given him when first taken captive was far worse than he'd thought.

Suddenly two men appeared at the doorway of the hut. They both held AKs on Solomon and ordered him to his feet.

"Fuck off. You want to kill me you do it here."

One of the ISWA men walked over to him and poked the gun barrel into his face and barked more orders. Solomon couldn't understand what he was saying but the meaning was plain. "Screw you, asshole," he growled.

The ISWA soldier brought his weapon

sweeping around and the butt smashed into the side of Solomon's head. He slumped sideways, stunned from the blow. His head swam and his vision blurred as he tried to fight off the enveloping darkness threatening to overwhelm him.

Rough hands grabbed the Delta commander's arms and started dragging him toward the door. He tried to fight with his remaining strength, but it was hopeless. Solomon was still stunned from the blow and his efforts were feeble.

Outside, the sun was hot and the flies thick. Men began to gather around to watch the proceedings. Through the blurred mist, Solomon looked for Falomo and his scimitar but couldn't find him.

The two men dropped him to the ground and Solomon's head bounced off the hard-packed earth. He groaned at the new pain that shot through his already pain-wracked head.

Boots crunched on fine gravel and stopped when the wearer loomed over the prone Delta man. Solomon dragged himself to his knees and sat back. He looked up at the man who stood over him with the scimitar, and growled, "Fuck you, asshole."

The curved blade was raised above the would-be killer's head. It began its downward arc when a 5.56 round reached out and punched into his brain.

"Suck on that, asshole," Axe growled, shifting his aim to burn down another terrorist. Shifted again and took out the third. "Three tangos down, Reaper."

"Everyone, move," Kane ordered the rest, impressed at his friend's skill with his SAW. They commenced searching for targets amongst the huts; Cara, still in control of the Raven working at locating them and Arenas calling them out.

"Bravo Six, you have a tango at your nine-o'clock about to appear from behind the hut."

Knocker swiveled to see the terrorist as he emerged from the space beside the shoddy building. He fired two shots before the man could get off a shot, dropping him silently at his feet. "Tango down."

Axe pressed forward toward the vulnerable Solomon. He knelt beside the prone figure and asked, "You good?"

The Delta man looked up and saw a big unshaven man wearing tactical gear beside him. "Where did you come from?"

"I'll tell you later. How many more of you?"

"One. Shane. He's in a bad way."

"Tell me your name."

"Ward Solomon, First Sergeant, Detachment Delta."

A figure with an AK appeared from behind one of the buildings to Axe's right. Reacting instantly, he fired a burst and the terrorist died. "Can you move?"

"I can fucking run if I have to."

"Let's start with walking and you can take me to Shane."

Kane and Brick circled around to the right where they found two more targets. Their suppressed 416s came to life and the pair of tangos jerked wildly before collapsing in a heap.

With the brutal efficiency of well-trained operators, they cleared the village, not allowing the ISWA terrorists a chance to fight back. Within ten minutes there wasn't a terrorist left alive.

"All callsigns report in," Kane said into his comms.

"Five OK."

"Six, OK."

"Reaper One this is Four. You'd best bring Brick with you. I think we're going to need a medevac."

Minutes later they had gathered outside the hut where Shane was being tended, waiting for Brick to finish his examination. Kane had called in the need for a medevac, but things did not look promising. "The nearest transport for you, Reaper, is at least two hours out," Ferrero told him grimly. "Since you have an airstrip close, we've sent the only thing available."

"What happened to the damned helo?"

"It got called away on an urgent mission. Like everything else. A SEAL Team has gotten themselves into trouble in Yemen. Troops in contact about to be overrun type of shit."

"Damn it."

"Say again your last, Reaper One."

"Roger that."

"I thought that's what you said. Can't be helped. I'm sorry but you're out in the middle of bum hump nowhere."

"That's bum fuck."

"Amen to that."

Kane turned to Solomon. "Care to fill me in while we wait?"

Solomon told Kane about the operation and then about being captured by Falomo. "He's a sadistic fuck," Solomon swore.

"Do you know where he went?"

"He left on the plane with the shipment of cocaine."

"Where to?"

"I don't know."

"Do you know what they were doing with it?"

Again, the Delta man shook his head. "No, but whatever it is, it isn't good."

Brick emerged from the hut. His face was a mask of concern. "We need to get him out of here as soon as possible. He's got internal bleeding and God knows what else. I got an IV into him but without proper care he won't make it."

"Two hours," was all Kane said.

"Two hours, what?"

"Until we get a bird in here to lift us all out."

"What happened to the extract chopper that was taking us out?"

"It seems something more important came up. Besides, they're getting a fixed-wing air-craft to come for us."

"How about this, his chances have gone from slim to fuck all."

"I'm sorry, Brick. Do what you can."

"It ain't much."

"Reaper Two, copy?" Kane said into his comms.

"Read you Lima Charlie, Reaper."

"What's your status?"

"We're recovering the Raven," she replied. "We'll head to you after we've done that."

"Roger that, see you when you get here."

Ten minutes later Cara and Arenas joined the rest of the team in the deserted village.

"What do we have?" Cara asked.

"We're just less than two hours from extract, the DEA man probably won't make it, and we're in the middle of Indian territory."

"What happened to our extract?"

"Don't ask."

Cara checked her weapon over and turned away from Kane. "Where you going?" he asked.

"Like you said, we're in the middle of Indian territory. I don't fancy being General Custer all the way out here."

# CHAPTER 14

*Camp Lemonnier, Djibouti*

"How long before the extract?" Thurston asked Ferrero.

The operations officer looked at his watch and said, "Approximately thirty minutes out."

"Any word on the casualty?"

"Last time I checked he was hanging in there."

The previous hour and a half had dragged slowly while everyone waited for the time of extract to arrive. What made it worse was the heat. The aircon was on the fritz and the ops center was fast becoming a sauna. Even with the fans turned on high. Things were going well; about as well as they could be when the team was out on a limb in the middle of hostile territory. But things have a tendency to go wrong, especially when things are going so right. This occasion was no exception.

"Zero we have a problem," Swift called across to Ferrero.

"What is it, Slick?"

"We have incoming vehicles from the north to the area of operations."

Ferrero started to feel his heart sink. "Put it on the big screen."

The satellite picture flashed up and the operations commander could see a line of trucks, some ten in all, rocketing along the road, kicking up a huge cloud of dust. "How far out are they?"

"Twenty minutes."

"Give the team a heads up. The more time they have to prepare, the better their chances will be."

"You're not telling them to pull out?" Thurston asked.

"And go where, Mary? If they get caught out in the open, they've got no chance. You know that."

The general nodded. She knew he was right but wanted to hear it. "All right. It means that the trucks will get there before the plane. They'll be on their own for at least ten minutes. I want to know if they can sustain heavy contact for that amount of time. Find an alternate exfil if we need it. Inform the C-one thirty captain that there's incoming to the LZ."

Ferrero turned to his people. "You heard the general. Get to it. Slick, do you have Kane on comms?"

"Working on it, Luis."

"Work faster."

**Niger, Africa**

"Reaper One, this is Bravo Four, copy?"

"Read you Lima Charlie, Bravo Four."

"You've got tangos inbound your position, Reaper One. Zero says for you to dig in."

Kane felt a sudden concern at the intel he was receiving. "How many and what direction, Bravo Four?"

"You have ten, that's one zero, trucks coming in from the north. There could be anywhere up to a hundred personnel in them. They will be at your position in approximately twenty minutes. Your extract will not be there for thirty. Zero would like to know if you have the ammunition to sustain solid contact for that time. Over."

Kane thought for a moment and said to Swift, "Stand by, Bravo Four." Then he said, "Reaper One to all callsigns. I need an ammo check, over."

The team reported in and Kane did some quick mental calculations. "Bravo Four, tell Zero that we should scrape through. The ammo is not my main concern."

"Understood, Reaper One. Good luck, out."

Yeah right. "All Reaper callsigns regroup on me ASAP. Acknowledge."

They all called in and within a couple of minutes had gathered around Kane's position. "Listen up, we've got anywhere up to a hundred tangos inbound in ten trucks. Looks like our ISWA friends are coming back."

Knocker chuckled. "You lot just attract trouble like flies to shit. I'm thinking I should have just shot my MI6 handler on the Queen and taken my chances."

"Too late to back out now," Axe said as he started to check his SAW.

Kane continued, "The trucks are coming in from the north. Cara, you need to find a hide somewhere."

"There's some high ground to the west which should give me a reasonably clear field of fire," she replied.

"Good get to it."

She jogged off and left the others to their decision making. "Brick, can we move Shane at all?"

"I'd advise against it. The only place he

should be going is aboard the medevac when it arrives."

Kane nodded. "We'll set up a strong point south of the crossroads in the village where we can fall back to after we initiate first contact to the north. We'll hit them out in the open, do as much damage as we can, and then fall back to the cover of the village so we can exfil to the east once our ride arrives."

Brick cleared his throat. "It would be easier to transport Shane, or any other wounded, if we had some wheels, Reaper."

He nodded. "It would be, but our wheels are three klicks out. Anyone here thinks they can get out there and back in under fifteen minutes?"

They looked at each other but it was Knocker who stepped forward. "Alright, fuck it. You blokes hold the fort while old Knocker puts his trainers on and goes for a run."

Axe shook his head. "He's talking brail again, Reaper."

"Sneakers, Axe."

"Oh."

"All right, Knocker. Drop your extra kit and do it. If you run into trouble, make sure you're back before we take off. The plane won't wait."

"Just don't start your kerfuffle without me," Knocker said. He looked around the group who stared back at him with blank expressions. He shook his head. "Remind me to give you blokes an English dictionary when we get back."

After the SAS man had disappeared Kane turned to the others. "Axe, set your SAW up with a good field of fire. I saw a mudbrick wall on the edge of town which should provide us with good cover. We hit them with the two-oh-threes first up and give them something to think about. Let's go."

"What about me?" Solomon asked.

Kane took his M17 and tossed it to the Delta man. Then a spare magazine. "Look after Shane. If they get through us, then—"

Kane didn't have to continue. "Yeah. Roger that."

They set up behind the mudbrick wall similar to the ones some of them had used for cover while touring Afghanistan. Axe had sited the SAW where he could sweep both sides of the battlefield with ease. But mostly he could shoot almost straight along the gravel road. From Cara's position, she could see the approach of the convoy of trucks. The billowing dust cloud thrown up into the hot sky resembled smoke signals from an old western movie, and as they drew closer, she could make out the vehicle shapes at the base of the cloud. Then they disappeared into a shallow depression only to reappear as they crested back out of it. "Reaper One target is approximately five mikes out."

"Roger that, Reaper Two. Any sign of Knocker?"

Cara turned and looked towards the direction the SAS man would come and saw another dust cloud. "I can see him Reaper. He'll arrive about the same time as the ISWA column."

"How's your hide, Cara?"

"It's surprisingly good. I have good cover from some rocks and my field of fire is wide."

"When the first truck is three hundred meters from the wall, I want you to take out the driver. That'll be our signal to fire the two-oh-threes," Kane told her. "The more open ground they have to cover the better. If any of the trucks try to flank us, try to shut them down. If they get in behind us, then our fallback position won't do us much good."

"I'll do what I can."

She settled down and waited, ticking off the distance in her head and checking her calculations until the convoy came into range. She sighted on the lead truck a battered old Mercedes Benz maybe built in the seventies, with a canopy over the back of it. It was a beast of a thing that had successfully survived the harshness dealt it by Africa. Until now.

Through her scope she could see two men sitting in front, the driver and his passenger, the latter was armed. The truck hit a deep rut and bounced across it before stabilizing. Cara let the vehicle come on a little further.

"Reaper One, this is Two."

"Go ahead, Two."

"I'm about to kick this thing off in three, two, one, sending."

Cara squeezed the trigger and the suppressed weapon slammed back against her shoulder. Through the scope she saw the driver jerk and then the truck swerve violently to the left before stopping. She shifted her aim to the second truck which was starting to turn away to the right, and put a round through its steer tire. The truck, another Mercedes rammed into the rear of the first.

The sudden violence caused a growing pile-up when the next three trucks in line concertinaed together.

It was then that the grenades from the 203s started to rain down upon the convoy and Axe commenced a steady spray with his SAW.

Geysers of debris shot skyward with each blast. One hit the lead truck, blowing the front of it apart. Flames shot from beneath the wrecked vehicle and out from behind it. Men started to tumble from the canopy-covered back, some with their clothes on fire. Cara ignored them and shifted her aim to the other trucks which were now disgorging their human load. One of them tried to go around the devastation in front of it, drawing Cara's attention. She sighted on the driver and sent a 7.62 round hurtling towards him at roughly seven hundred and eighty meters per second. It punched through the glass of the front window and smashed into his head, bringing his attempted escape to a bloody and shuddering halt.

More of the forty-millimeter grenades fell from the sky and Cara saw one of the terrorists thrown bodily from his feet by the blast. He fell in a heap, his weapon beside him and he never moved.

From the rear of the column another truck tried to do the same thing and pulled from the line and off the road. "Stop right there, you son of a bitch," Cara whispered to herself and fired the CSASS.

Her aim was off a touch and the bullet spiderwebbed the window of the truck between the passenger and the driver. She adjusted with a soft curse and fired again. This time the slug burned deep into the terrorist's chest and took away his life, the truck slowing to a stop.

From the back of the remaining trucks, ISWA soldiers appeared and dropped to the ground. They crawled on their bellies away from the vehicles as fast as they could, trying to avoid the grenades that continued raining down.

Cara's work was methodical as she picked her targets and dispatched them into the afterlife. Some would say it was like shooting fish in a barrel. And it was until the terrorists woke up to the fact that staying in the open, was an invitation to death. That was when they clambered to their feet and charged toward the wall where the others were sheltered.

It took Knocker longer than he anticipated to get the yellow taxi van started. At first, he thought he was doing something wrong, but then worked out that the big yellow bitch was like his first wife; stubborn and trying to screw him over. When he finally got the damned thing running it never missed a beat.

As he approached the town, he could see that the engagement had already started. "Bollocks," he growled at being late for the party. "Reaper One, this is Six. I'm coming in from the south. Don't shoot me."

"Better late than never, Reaper Six. Thought

you must have skived off," Kane said throwing some of the SAS man's English back at him.

"Skived off, my fat aunt's fucking ass. This piece of tosh decided it wanted to act like my first wife."

"Piece of what?" Kane asked and Knocker could hear the gunfire in the background.

"Shit, you wanker. Christ!"

"Why didn't you say so? We're about to fall back. Park behind one of the buildings on the southside of the crossroads."

"Copy. Will do. Out."


Kane fired another forty-millimeter grenade at the oncoming terrorist horde and then started in on them with the 416. Beside him Axe still had the SAW churning out lead like an ammunition factory. Brick and Arenas were further along the wall and working with methodical ease as the ISWA soldiers surged forward.

Kane ducked behind the wall, return fire slamming into it. He pressed the talk button on his comms and asked, "How long before our extract arrives, Zero?"

"Reaper One, extract is still five minutes out."

"Roger," Kane acknowledged. "All Reaper callsigns pull back to the strongpoint. Cara, you too."

The four shooters behind the wall came to their feet and, keeping low to avoid the bullets flying overhead, made their way back into the village. The strong point, as it was called, was more of a position. They would use the huts for cover and wait while the terrorists were funneled toward them.

"You blokes look like you've been busy," Knocker greeted them when they appeared. "Your friends coming for a visit?"

"They'll be here directly," Axe informed him.

Brick took a minute to check on Shane and was relieved to find him still alive. Cara came in from her hide and joined them just as the ISWA soldiers began streaming in from the north. At a rough estimate, Kane figured there might be somewhere between eighty or ninety of them still alive.

They joined the battle again in earnest, and once more, the atmosphere was filled with flying lead. Chunks of mud were hammered from the huts and fell to create mounds of it at the base of the walls. An explosion rocked the village and a cloud of flame and smoke billowed into the air. "They've got grenades, Reaper!" Brick shouted.

Another explosion, this one closer than the last and Kane could hear and see the debris falling to the ground around him. Suddenly the shout of, "Man down!" rang out. "Who is it?" Kane asked into his mic.

"It's Carlos," came the reply from Brick.

"Can you get to him?"

"No, I'm pinned down."

"I can get him," Knocker said. "Just give me some cover fire."

The team's rate of fire picked up and the SAS man broke cover. He ran across to Arenas who still lay prone on the ground and grasped the Mexican by the collar to drag him behind the hut.

"Reaper, watch your left, they're trying to circle around behind us," Cara's voice called a warning.

Kane turned and saw the two ISWA men who appeared to be doing just that. His 416 came up and he squeezed the trigger six times. Both men fell to the dusty ground and never moved. "Knocker, how's Carlos?"

"He'll be OK. Just had the shit bashed out of him."

The Team Reaper commander felt a wave of relief wash over him, but it quickly dissipated when a torrent of bullets came in from the south.

"Reaper, they're behind us!" Brick shouted.

"How many?"

"Five or six."

"Put them down. Knocker have you finished?"

"Yeah, Carlos is back on his feet."

"Help Brick clean out those bastards behind us," Kane growled.

"On it."

The rate of incoming fire seemed to grow exponentially as the terrorists pushed in closer. They seemed to be behind every rock and hut north of the strongpoint. And now they were getting in behind them. The only thing holding them back was the superior firepower of the SAW. Without it they would be screwed. If it—

Axe ran out of ammunition.

"Fucking son of a bitch!" the ex-recon marine snarled as he dropped the weapon and grabbed his M17.

"Tell me you have a jam, Axe," Kane called out.

"Out of ammo, Reaper," he shouted back putting two slugs in the chest of an oncoming ISWA soldier.

With a weary realization, Kane knew that there was a real possibility that the team could be overrun at any moment. "Zero, where's the damned extract?"

Before the reply could come back across the

airwaves, a huge bird flew low overhead with an ear-pounding roar. "Reaper One this is Stinger One-One, how copy? Over."

Kane looked up at the beautiful big AC-130 as it passed, and saw something which made his heart pound.

The AC-130 Spooky II was armed with a five barreled 25mm rotary cannon, a 40mm Bofors cannon, and a 105mm M102 Howitzer. In reality, to ground troops about to be overwhelmed and in need, the beast looked like a flying battleship. Good old Luis. Stinger One-One this is Reaper One. Read you Lima Charlie. Damned good to see you."

"Glad we could make it on time, Reaper One. Give me a target and I'll have my guys and gals start pounding some terrorist ass for you."

"Roger that, Stinger. Any target north of the village crossroads you can consider hostile. I say again, any target north of the crossroads. Danger close, I repeat, danger close. Over."

"Good copy, Reaper One. Danger close north of the crossroads. Hold onto your hats, Stinger One-One inbound and going hot."

Kane then said to his team, "Everyone keep your heads down. Fire mission inbound."

The AC-130 took up a circular holding pattern and started to unleash hell on the ISWA soldiers to the team's north. The rotary cannon rent the air as deadly lances reached out, destroying everything they touched. The other weapon elected for use by the fire control officer was the Bofors. It was a solid weapon for danger close missions because of its limited risk of collateral damage unlike the 105. It could also fire up to one-hundred rounds per minute.

The ground appeared to erupt beneath the onslaught of fire, and the IWA soldiers seemed to dissolve beneath the deadly rain. Within moments the attack turned into a rout and the terrorists turned tail and ran.

"Reaper One, this is Stinger One-One. Looks like your friends are bugging out. We'll give them one more pass and then put this bird down so we can pick y'all up."

"Copy, Stinger. We'll be ready."

With their incoming fire non-existent, Kane stood and turned to Brick who'd rejoined them. "Get Shane ready and tell Solomon he can come out now."

"I'm already here."

Kane stared at him. "You all good?"

"Yeah."

"Give Brick a hand."

The Delta man nodded and went off with the ex-SEAL. "I'll go get our transport," Knocker said. "Might be easier to transport our casualty."

"Do it."

Cara stepped up beside Kane. "You OK?" she asked.

He nodded. "Tired. You?"

"I'm so jacked up on juice I'm going to need a man to take it out on."

Kane gave her a wry smile. "Sing out if you can't find anyone."

"Remember the whole teammate thing?"

"I just quit."

"Frig off," she chuckled knowing that if they weren't in the situation, they found themselves in she'd jump at the opportunity in a heartbeat. "No intel but it was a good outcome."

"Yes. Two hostages saved is always a good outcome. As for intel, we have one solid lead."

Cara looked at him confused for a moment and then realized what he was getting at. "The South African. Botha."

"That's him. He's in this somehow, we just have to work out how."

"I'm not looking forward to getting back to Djibouti," Cara said.

"Why's that?"

"Fredericks."

"You're right," Kane moaned. "Maybe he'll be gone when we touch down."

"Don't bet on it."

# CHAPTER 15

*Camp Lemonnier, Djibouti*

"Good to see you back in one piece, Reaper," Traynor called across to Kane as he entered the ops room, wearing only his pants and a towel draped over his shoulders. With each movement his defined muscles rippled. He smiled at the ex-DEA man and said, "It's good to be back. That damned shower was like heaven."

"I'm glad to see you back safely too, Mister Kane."

"Mister Fredericks, you're still here. I thought you'd be gone home by now."

The man shrugged. "Not yet. I still have a job to complete."

Kane sighed. "How about we cut to the chase, Mister Fredericks? It's me you want to talk to not the others. Only I can give you the answers you want."

The justice department man nodded. "It would save us a lot of time and energy."

The attention of all those present in the ops center was suddenly drawn to the two men and Kane was aware of it. "Come with me, Mister Fredericks."

Kane took him to a small room where they could speak, privately. They sat down in a couple of chairs and were just about to get started when Thurston entered. "You want me for something, ma'am?"

She shook her head. "No. Just making sure you're not going to flush your career down the toilet."

"I'll be fine, General."

"I don't much care what you think. Is it all right if I sit in, Mister Fredericks?"

"Please do, General Thurston. I have no objection."

Thurston grabbed a chair and sat next to Kane. "You could have at least put a shirt on."

"Just got out of the shower, ma'am. Been on a mission."

"Shall we get started?" Fredericks asked, placing a small recorder from his pocket on the table in front of them.

"What do you want to know?"

"What happened in Australia? After all, that

is what started all of this."

Kane thought for a moment and said, "I did what I had to do to keep my team and myself alive."

"By stabbing the complainant?"

"Complainant, my ass," Kane muttered. "He's a top-ranked cartel boss responsible for the deaths of a whole lot of people."

"Yes, I understand that, but it doesn't mean you can stab—"

"I didn't stab him. I surgically removed the offending item."

"What would that have been?"

"A tracker."

"A tracker?"

"Yes, a tracker. You do know what a tracker is, don't you?" Kane asked testily. He felt Thurston's hand touch his thigh under the table but never looked in her direction.

"Yes, Mister Kane, I do know what a tracker is."

"Well then, you can understand our dilemma, can't you?"

Fredericks shook his head. "Not really. How about you tell me."

"We were outnumbered by militia. They were closing in on us and the reason was, Laso had a tracker in his leg and that's how they were doing it. To leave it there would have signed our death warrants."

"So, you stabbed—"

"I didn't fucking stab him," Kane grated, the veins on his neck standing out.

Stunned by Kane's anger, the Justice man rephrased the question. "And you decided to remove the offending object?"

"It was either that or die."

"How are we to know that there was a tracker as you claim? After all, there is only your word for it."

Kane's eyes narrowed. "What did you say?"

"Reaper," Thurston cautioned.

"Mister Kane, what I'm saying is that there is no proof of the tracker ever existing. Mister Laso denies there ever being one. If you can come up with the proof of there being one, then that's great because at the moment, you are looking at a charge of torturing a prisoner."

Kane leaped to his feet, the chair tipping backwards onto the floor as he did so. "What the f—"

"What kind of BS is this?" Thurston demanded.

"I'm not saying that there wasn't one, General. In fact, I'd probably believe your man before anyone else but what I think doesn't matter. There has to be proof or I'm afraid Mister Kane will be looking at serious charges."

"This is horseshit," Kane growled.

"Do you have the tracker?"

"No."

"Do you have anything at all?"

"I have recordings of radio chatter from the mission," Thurston said. "It will show Kane asking about any radio frequencies in the immediate area and our tech picking one up. If need be, he will testify to it being a transmission from a tracker."

Fredericks nodded. "That's better than what you had a minute ago. Is there anything else?"

"Only that and the fact the militia stopped chasing us when the tracker was thrown away," Kane said.

"Did any of your team see the tracker?" the Justice man asked.

Kane shook his head.

"Well it's not a lot, Mister Kane, but it's more than what you had," Fredericks allowed. He leaned forward and turned the recorder off. "And off the record, I believe you and I'll do whatever I can to help, but once I file the report it's out of my hands. I've seen what you people do first-hand and I must say I'm glad I sit behind a desk. The world needs more teams like yours to take on the drug problem, a problem that we're losing. Maybe, just maybe, some other countries will follow your lead and take the problem head-on. I take no joy in doing this, Mister Kane, but it is a job that must be done. Thank you for giving me the time."

The justice man held out his hand. "I'll understand if you slap it away."

Kane surprised both him and Thurston by taking it. "I understand that you have a job to do, Mister Fredericks and it's one I wouldn't want either. I'm more at home where the bullets are flying and we're making a difference. I agree with you that we're still losing the war on drugs, but maybe one day it will all turn around and we'll get the upper hand. It's something we have to believe that will happen or we'd all just give up and give them the victory."

"Good luck, Mister Kane. I'll be headed back to DC when I can. I'll do what I can for you."

"That's all I ask."

When Fredericks left the room, Kane turned to Thurston. "What do you think?"

She shrugged. "I don't know what to think. Hopefully that will be the end of it. I'll pull everything he needs and give it to him personally before he flies out."

"Thanks, General."

"Can't have my best operator leaving the team because of some asshole, can I?" Thurston stated.

"How is Shane doing? Have you heard?"

"Not yet, too early. Brick said he was surprised he lasted as long as he did. How did your SAS man go?"

Kane gave her a broad smile.

"What's so funny?"

"The language barrier between Knocker and the others."

"That good?"

His smile broadened. "Even better."

"Get some rest. I want a full debrief tomorrow and we'll work out where to from there."

"Paul Botha is the key. He did something to the cocaine, and we need to find out what."

"You want to run an op down there?"

"We might have to."

"Think it over and I'll see if I can get clearance. In the meantime, sleep."

"Yes, ma'am."


"Mister Jensen, it would seem that your commanding officer has allowed us to keep you for a while. Any objection?" Thurston asked the SAS operator.

"I have one," Axe called out from where he was seated.

"What would that be, Axel?" the words were almost groaned out of the general's mouth.

"Are you mad at me, ma'am? Did I do something wrong?"

"No, Axel, why do you ask?"

"It's just that every time you call me Axel I—"

"The objection, Axe? What is it?"

"Oh, right. Um, he can't speak American and I can't understand him for shit."

"This country will not be a good place for any of us to live in unless we make it a good place for all of us to live in."

Axe looked confused. "What?"

"You don't understand American either."

The ex-recon marine leaned close to Kane. "What did she say?"

"It was a quote by Roosevelt."

"Oh."

Knocker said, "Just brilliant, ma'am, I've got bugger all else to do, I guess. Better than skiving off somewhere. She'll be hunky-dory."

"See what I mean," Axe said.

Knocker winked at Kane and gave him a smile.

"All right, let's get down to business," Thurston said. "First thing, we have no idea where Falomo and the second shipment of cocaine went. I reached out to the CIA and they are shaking a few trees."

"What about the link to Mexico, ma'am?" Cara asked.

"It's still there. We just have to find something solid."

"So, our only real lead is Paul Botha," Ferrero continued. A picture of the South African came up on a large screen. He left with the first shipment and is a bioengineer, which is a good start. However, there is a fly in the ointment, the South African President, Sonja Petersen, is his daughter."

An uncertain murmur ran around the room. Ferrero continued. "She is the first white president since apartheid disappeared. Needless to say, that she's not going to let us on South African soil, especially if it involves her father. We did a little digging on Botha and have come up with links to a white supremacist group called The Children of the New South Africa."

"What about his daughter?" Cara asked.

"The ties to white supremacy go back a way so she could possibly know about them. What makes us think that she could have ties is she is currently trying to disband the three-capital system and go with one. That would be in Johannesburg."

Kane sat and thought for a moment studying the picture of Botha. Thurston saw his expression and asked, "What are you thinking?"

His gaze flicked to her. "White supremacist with a possible white supremacist daughter. He's a biological engineer with a load of cocaine. Where is the largest population for cocaine dependence in South Africa?"

"Slick?" Thurston asked their computer tech.

A few keystrokes later and he said, "Johannesburg."

"Where?"

"Soweto."

"Where is Paul Botha based again?"

"Johannesburg."

The general turned back to Kane who nodded slowly. "What was Sonja Petersen elected on?"

"The main reform she proposed was to clean up the drug problem in South Africa. Starting with the problem in Soweto," Swift told him.

"What better way to do it than with juiced up cocaine. Cure the problem by eliminating it."

Swift frowned as he looked at his computer screen. He tapped a few keys and frowned some more. "I'm seeing a slight problem with the figures I'm looking at."

"What is it?" Thurston asked.

"The figures for the Soweto drug problem. They were steady until two years ago when they jumped exponentially. Almost tripled in fact."

"Why would they do that?" Axe asked.

"So, they can draw attention to the problem and give them an excuse," Cara said.

"Excuse for what?"

It was Brick who said it first. "They lace the cocaine and all the real drug-addicted blacks start to die. The deaths mount up and then they move in and clean it out probably using military force."

"But that will cause a riot," Cara said.

"And what better excuse for racial genocide?" Kane said. "The military starts getting attacked and they open fire."

"I don't think it will be military," Swift said.

All eyes turned to the red-headed technician. "Continue, Mister Swift," Thurston said suddenly sounding official.

"The South African government just hired a security firm called Roman Legion Security."

"I know those bastards," Knocker said. "They're British mob. They first showed up in Afghanistan in oh-eight. Lot of bad shit dragged along with them. Some of their men were blamed for shooting prisoners. They were accused of dealing in drugs and arms. One time it was said that they sold guns to some Afghanis and then shot them down."

"Right bunch of assholes," Brick said.

"And then some."

"So, we think we know who and why," Ferrero said. "We just don't know how."

"Technically we do," Kane said. "They're

going to do something to the cocaine."

"But what?"

"That we don't know."

"Then we're going to find out," Thurston said.

"Does that mean we're sending a team?" Cara asked.

Thurston nodded. "Yes. A small team. The rest of us will stay here."

"Who's going?" Kane asked.

"I will," said Ferrero. "And Slick. You and Cara plus one more."

"Count me in," said Knocker. "I'm not missing out on this do."

They all looked at him. "Oh, for crying out loud. A party? Festivities?"

"Why not just say an op?" Axe asked.

"All right, Jensen is the third person. You have any objections, Reaper?" Thurston asked.

"No, none at all."

"Remember, this will be an unsanctioned operation. We need to be darker than black. I'll get intel from the CIA and have it waiting at their safe house when you arrive. Slick will put it together along with anything else you need to know and brief you before you go in."

"Just where is it, we're going in to?" Cara asked.

A picture came up of a large square building.

"This is Botha Pharmaceuticals. It is based in Johannesburg. This is where our target works. As you can see from the picture it also has a large fence and armed guards. Motion sensors as well and armed response teams."

"We're meant to go in there?" Kane asked.

Thurston shrugged. "It is one option. The second is his home."

Swift changed the picture and a large mansion popped up. Two floors, large fence, more armed guards.

"That looks just as bad," Cara observed.

"I prefer the third option," Knocker said.

"And what would that be?" Ferrero asked the SAS man.

"We snatch him in transit."

"Might work," Kane said. "Do we have anything on him coming to and from work?"

"No, but by the time we get to Johannesburg we should."

Satisfied with that Kane nodded. "When do we leave?"

"Wheels up in two hours," Ferrero told him. "We'll fly to Mozambique and the CIA will get us into South Africa. Handguns only. Bring suppressors and vests. That's it. Go and get your kit together."

# CHAPTER 16

*Johannesburg, South Africa*

The CIA safehouse wasn't exactly a house as such. It was a large warehouse on the outskirts of the city. The building had once been a part of a manufacturing complex and was surrounded by other similar warehouses each with paint peeling from their structures, rusted girders, broken windows, plus walls tagged with graffiti. The grounds on which it stood were overgrown by trees and grass which hid it rather well from the road. Even better to keep prying eyes out. Even parts of the structures were removed to make it look like shack people had been robbing bits from it for shelter.

The team arrived in two white Toyota SUVs driven by CIA officers whose names were Bert

Sacks and Ryan Mertens. Mertens was middle-aged with twenty years' experience and the younger Sacks had ten.

The inside of the building belied its looks. A large open-plan operations room was staffed by at least six officers, a mix of women and men. It was like a building within a building.

"How long have you been here?" Ferrero asked Sacks.

"Two years. Ever since the Presidency changed over," he explained.

"You obviously have some misgivings?" Ferrero inquired.

"She's her father's daughter," Sacks said. "She may look all prim and proper on the outside. All stately, but behind the scenes she has an agenda and her own personal moordspan or murder squad."

"So, the apple doesn't fall far from the tree," Kane said.

"Last week a journalist died when his car blew up. We think he was getting close to something happening in Soweto. And judging what we now know from your findings, it's all tied together."

"Which is why we need to get to Botha. He's connected somehow to Abadi Falomo and did something for him concerning another shipment of cocaine," Ferrero explained. "We think the shipment is headed for Mexico to a cartel run by Amaya Caro. If it is, then we can guess the next stop. Continental United States. We need to find out what he's done to it and anything else."

"ISWA Abadi Falomo?"

"Yes."

"Well, you'd best get started. We have placed all the intel we gathered on the table over there." Sacks pointed toward a large table in the corner of the room. "If you need anything else let us know."

"We'll need transport," Kane said. "Preferably an SUV. Maybe two."

"I'll fix it."

"Thank you."

They walked over to the table and sat down. In the center of the laminate surface was a pile of folders containing papers and pictures. Ferrero passed them out to the others, and they went to work.

It was well after dark when they finally finished and began to fashion together a kind of plan. "Are we agreed?" Kane asked.

"Yes," they all said with a nod. The plan was to take Botha in transit between his home and work. It would still be risky due to his escort having been changed in recent times to Roman Legion Security. There were three vehicles in the convoy. Botha always rode in the center one with two bodyguards. In the other two SUVs provided by the security firm were two additional teams of two. A total of six body-guards who appeared to be well-armed with M6A2s and handguns.

The plan was to take out the two escort vehicles without hurting the middle one. It would also involve some collateral damage, namely the escorts. "I don't like the idea of killing those in the escort vehicles just to get at Botha," Kane said aloud. "But I don't see a way around it."

"The wankers shouldn't work for assholes like Roman Legion, then should they?" Knock-er said. "But if it's going to upset you that much, then I think I can find a way around it."

"How?" asked Cara.

"I've run enough escorts to know that they'll be moving quick and compact. So, placing the charges in the road shouldn't be an issue. I'll just lessen the blast. It'll still knock them around a bit, but it shouldn't kill them. Just give us enough time to get Botha."

"You're forgetting the two with him," Fer-rero pointed out. "They'll come out shooting."

"I didn't say the plan was perfect."

"They wear vests," Kane pointed out. "If we hit them hard enough, it should put them out of the fight long enough for us to capture the package. Killing them is a last resort."

"That's a dangerous game, Reaper," Knocker said.

The Team Reaper commander nodded. "It is but if this goes sideways, I don't want to be staring down the barrel of multiple murder charges. At least that way someone might be able to get us out."

"That's a load of bollocks," Knocker snorted.

"I thought it sounded positive. You're right though, if we get caught, we're screwed," Kane said with a wry smile. "We go in the morning. Get some rest."

When the others walked off Kane was left with Ferrero. "If this gets too much at any time, John just waved it off."

Kane studied his operations commander's face. He could see the worry there. "We'll be fine," he tried to reassure him. "In and out."


"I'm beginning to think that you are another Axe, Reaper," Cara called out as she blew off three rounds from her M17.

"Shut up and shoot, woman," he growled

from behind his facemask which they all wore. Kane's was that of a skull, Cara was Minnie Mouse, and somehow Knocker had managed to score one of Prince Charles.

"Does this shit happen a lot?" Knocker asked as he reloaded his handgun.

"Only every other day," Cara said. "You should have learned from Nigeria."

The SAS man rose up and fired across the hood of the SUV. "Thought it was a one-off, love."

"Oh, no, this sort of shit happens all the time."

"It should have been fucking picked up," Kane growled.

In the background one of the escort vehicles burned while the third was on its side. The initial part of the plan had worked perfectly. The two escorts were taken out and the SUV with Botha inside had been stopped. The driver and other bodyguard had climbed out and the team had put them down without any drama. Then came the third escort vehicle. A black BMW sedan with four more men in it.

That was the beginning of their trouble. They'd arrived just as Knocker was pulling a protesting Botha from the rear of his ride. A handgun was on the street, no doubt Botha's personal weapon. As soon as the newcomers had climbed from the BMW, they opened fire. Cara had called, "Contact rear!" and then engaged. There was no time to be picky with placement and her first shots had hit one of the shooters in the chest and then in the face. She'd cursed under her breath when the remainder opened fire with their M6A2s and bullets started to stitch the air around her.

"Where did they come from?" Kane had cried out before getting onto his comms. "Zero we've got a problem. A third escort vehicle has arrived with four more tangos. Correction, make that three."

"Roger, Reaper One, we're seeing it on ISR. You need to get your package out of there immediately before you have Johannesburg police and more contractors crawling all over you."

"No shit," Kane whispered.

They had swapped bullets with the security contractor for a few minutes more before Cara had told him if he was another Axe. Kane looked about and saw that they were getting nowhere. Now they were pinned down behind the SUV which had been carrying Botha and in deep shit.

"We need to pull back to the –" Knocker started but his words were cut off as bullets hammered the vehicle.

"These guys don't seem to be too worried

about Botha, Reaper," Cara said.

Suddenly he realized that she was right. The shooters didn't give a damn. They were just pouring fire into the vehicle they sheltered behind. Kane shifted position and crouched beside Botha who leaned against a back wheel, his hands cable-tied together. "Hey, what's going on? Why don't they care if they kill you?"

The man didn't answer, just sat there as though he had total acceptance and peace with the situation. Then it clicked, they were trying to kill him, and he knew it.

"Why are they trying to kill you?" Kane asked him, voice raised over the gunfire.

Still no answer.

This time the Team Reaper commander slapped Botha across the face. "Why, damn it?"

The Bio man looked up and glared at Kane. "My daughter. I cannot be left alive for her secret to get out. So, I am to die. Fucking bitch."

"What secret?"

A flurry of shots from Cara and Knocker made Botha pause before he spoke again. "The purification of Johannesburg."

"What has she got planned?"

"You blokes want to hurry the fuck up," Knocker growled. "These pricks are getting serious."

"What has she got planned, Botha."

"We are – she is going to rid Soweto of the blacks. Once they are gone it will be bulldozed and rebuilt."

"How? What is in the cocaine?"

The man's eyes reflected the realization of the fact that the plan was starting to unravel. "It is cut with anthrax."

"Jesus Christ," Kane hissed. "Is the same stuff going to the US?"

Botha opened his mouth to speak when a round smashed into his head and the words were never uttered. "Fuck!" Kane shouted. "Sniper, move!"

Another round came whistling in, but Kane had moved and the bullet punched into the body of the SUV. "Time to go."

The three of them kept their heads down and ran for the SUV they'd used. Cara scrambled into the driver's seat and turned the key. By the time the others had climbed in she'd shifted the stick into drive and planted her foot on the gas.

The windows shattered as the security team turned assassins let rip another burst of fire. "Will you guys shoot back?"

Knocker sat in the back and fired ten rounds from his seventeen-round magazine at the shooters through the now glassless window. He dropped out the empty mag and replaced it with another. What did he say?"

"Who?" Kane called back. As the SUV slid around a corner, its tires squealing on the asphalt.

"You know who, mate."

"Nothing much really. Just that it was his daughter trying to kill him and that she was trying to clean out Soweto with anthrax-laced cocaine."

"The silly fucking cow," Knocker growled.

"Is that what's going to Amaya Caro?" Cara asked.

"No idea. We never got that far," Kane said and then into his comms, "Zero, Reaper One."

"Go ahead, Reaper One."

"We've managed to get away, but we're light one package. They were there to kill him, over."

"Why?"

"Because the daughter didn't want it to get out what they were up to. They're going to clean out Soweto starting with anthrax-laced cocaine."

"Repeat your last, Reaper One."

"You heard me right, Luis. Anthrax-laced cocaine."

"Do we have confirmation on that Reaper?"

"I got it from the horse's mouth, Luis. Right before he died."

"Anything on the second shipment, Reaper

One?" Ferrero asked.

"Negative, Zero."

"Roger that. Return to base."

"You need to find out where that shipment is being held, Luis," Thurston said. "And then destroy it."

"And what do we do about Sonja Petersen?" Ferrero asked the screen.

"I'll let Hank know what we've got, and he can kick it upstairs to the president. Your main focus is the anthrax."

Ferrero nodded. "Don't forget the other shipment. It's a reasonably safe bet that it's the same one that Flores was talking about. What makes it worse is that I think Falomo is with it. This could be a terrorist attack of epic proportions once that shit gets on the street."

"I agree. I'm going to send Carlos and Pete Traynor to Mexico to work with Flavia Ojeda. We need to see if they can scrape together some intel. Once we're done in Johannesburg, then we can fly out for there."

"We?" Ferrero asked.

"The rest of the team and myself will be there by evening. Find out where that cocaine is, Luis. And do it in a hurry."

Thurston signed off and Ferrero turned to

Swift. "Find me something, Slick. Anything will do."

"On it, boss."

Ferrero turned to Sacks and asked, "If you wanted to get a load of cocaine into the city, how would you do it?"

"Botha was well known to ship pharmaceuticals to poorer countries to help their flagging medical supplies."

Ferrero frowned. "A white supremacist helping out predominantly black countries with medical aid?"

"It was part of his cover."

"For what?"

"We think, can't prove it, that the medical supplies were below strength. Like if it was antibiotics for some diseases that they sent to say, Uganda, the drugs would be well below full strength or substituted with flour so they would be ineffective. However, the proper stuff would be mixed amongst it so that some would survive while others would die."

"Calculating son of a bitch," Ferrero said.

"So's his daughter," Sacks allowed.

"If he could get drugs out then no one would suspect what would be in a shipment coming in marked as medical supplies."

Sacks nodded. "Most likely not."

"Slick, we need to know where Botha keeps

his medical supplies."

"I'll see what I can do."

Ten minutes later a video call came through to the warehouse from Melissa Smith. "Luis, is your man there with you?" she asked.

"Just one moment, Melissa, I'll have someone get him."

"Thank you."

Two more minutes passed and Kane was standing alongside Ferrero. "You wanted me, ma'am?"

"I wanted to hear first-hand about the threat to the South African people. I'll brief the president in an hour. Hank Jones filled me in on what Mary Thurston had reported to him."

"It amounts to genocide, ma'am," Kane informed her and then went on to tell Melissa about what Botha had told him.

"What are you doing about it, Luis?" she asked Ferrero.

"We're trying to track down the cocaine. We have an idea how he got it into the country. Our main problem will be Sonja Petersen and her new security."

"Let me know if you need anything."

"We could use some biohazard suits."

"Have Sacks get you some. We should have them somewhere. Always handy just in case Ebola decides to rear its ugly head. By the way, use my people any way you see fit. Just get this stopped. I've already sent word to my people to start sniffing around in Mexico. If Falomo is headed there with more of the biothreat then we need to contain it on the Mexican side. Good luck."

"Thank you, Melissa."

Ferrero turned to Kane. "Get some rest. As soon as we find the cocaine, you'll be headed back out."

"What's going on in Mexico?" Kane asked.

"Mary is sending Carlos and Traynor to gather intel with Ojeda. Once we're finished here then we'll join them. I think between them and the CIA they should be able to dig up something."

**Ovarro City, Mexico**
**Thirty-six hours later**

"Amaya Caro has disappeared," Ojeda said to Traynor. "Turned into a ghost."

Traynor frowned. "Why would she do that?"

"Maybe your commander is right. Maybe they are up to something and have disappeared until after it happens."

"There must be a way we can find her?"

Ojeda shrugged. "I can put out some feelers to see what I can come up with, but it will probably be fruitless."

Traynor turned to Arenas. "What about you? You know how these people think."

"Officer Ojeda is right. She has gone to ground until after whatever is planned happens."

"That means the cocaine is in the country and possibly Falomo," Traynor theorized. There's only one thing for it. I need to speak to some old friends."

Arenas nodded. "I will go with you."

"Where are you going?" Ojeda asked.

"Mexico City. I know a guy there who was deep in the Messinas Cartel. Probably still is."

"If he is, then you both could end up dead before you get close to him," Ojeda said.

"I can get close to him. Getting away might be another problem."

"You seem to forget the most important thing in this whole equation," the Mexican intelligence officer stated. "The Messinas Cartel was taken over by Amaya Caro."

Traynor smiled at her. "That's why I'm going to see him. The guy I know is Carlo Messinas. The son of Eduardo Messinas. I'm hoping he harbors a little animosity towards his new boss."

"You live dangerously my friend," Arenas said.

"It was a whole other life, Carlos. I was undercover for a long time. But if anyone knows something, Carlo will."

"Let's hope so. If the cocaine gets out in America a lot of people will die."

# CHAPTER 17

*Johannesburg, South Africa*

The excitement on Swift's face said it all. Once Ferrero saw it, he asked, "Where?"

"Witwatersrand. It is a suburb of Johannesburg. There's a large estate there owned by— care to take a guess?"

"Sonja Petersen?"

"Got it in one."

"Shit. Get the others, you can fill us all in at the same time. And then we can work out what the hell we're going to do about it."

A few minutes later Kane, Cara, Knocker, and Sacks were gathered around a table and waiting for Swift to tell them what he knew. He hit a key on his notebook computer and spun it around, the screen revealing a picture of a single level mansion on lush grounds. "This is

Witwatersrand. It is a suburb of Johannesburg and is owned by Sonja Petersen."

"Well, fuck me. It's a rainy day in Scotland," Knocker growled. "You're like that gray cloud that hangs overhead waiting to piss down on those underneath it."

"It gets better," Swift said with a smile. "It's guarded by those Legion wankers."

The British SAS man smiled. "Maybe you're not a bad bloke after all. "You see anything dodgy, mate?"

"What?"

Knocker shook his head. "I knew it was too good to be true."

"It's set on five acres," Swift continued. "The perimeter is patrolled day and night. I managed—"

"How many?" Kane asked, interrupting.

"Fifteen. Not all at one time."

"Enough, then. Is the fence electrified?"

"I'm not sure. But it would be best if you assume it is. If so, we can work the problem with you onsite."

Kane nodded and allowed the tech to continue. "As I was saying, I managed to track what I assume is the drug shipment to this estate. The dates line up and the truck that entered the gates was the only one in the past month and a half."

"Where are they storing the stuff?" Cara asked.

Swift changed a picture and another building came up. "There is a large barn on the east side of the main building. That was where it was unloaded. There are two guards outside the building at all times."

"It's a safe bet then," Knocker said.

"Almost certain," Ferrero agreed.

"What's the plan, Luis?" Kane asked. "If we get caught, we're screwed beyond all recognition. We'll be called terrorists if we're lucky. More than likely classed as assassins who tried to kill the President of South Africa. It won't matter if she's not there. She'll spin it to her advantage."

"Agreed. There'll be no half measures. You'll go in full tactical. Find the drugs and blow them. The only way it can be done is with incendiary devices. You'll need to wear biohazard suits as well."

"What's our ROEs?" Knocker asked.

"There are no rules. You do what you have to do to accomplish the mission. Understood?"

"Lima Charlie," Kane answered.

Ferrero looked at Sacks. "Your boss told me I could rely on you for some things we might need. Can you supply the suits and weapons, and other things like the explosives?"

"Give me a list and I'll have it for you by dark."

"Thank you. Reaper, work up a plan. You go tonight."

"Roger that."


Sonja Petersen saw the last of the mourners out and turned to face Grady Turner. "Tell me what the fuck happened," she hissed in her deep Afrikaans accented voice.

"We've been able to piece a little together since it happened, Madam President," the big dark-haired Roman Legion Security boss told her. "From cameras and such but their identity is still unknown. Whoever they were I'm reasonably sure that they were professionals and that their objective was to kidnap your father."

"Do you think they know about the plans my father and I had?"

"It is hard to say. But even if they do, they would never find it because your father didn't know where it was taken after it arrived in Johannesburg."

"We cannot risk it, nor I the scandal," Sonja said. Her fine-featured face turned hard; her blue eyes sparked with anger. "Fuck them whoever they are. We shift the cocaine tomorrow and then start to distribute it in Soweto.

My plans must not stop now."

One of Sonja's aides appeared in the doorway of the living room, a phone in her hand. She had a confused expression on her face. "What is it?" the president growled.

"A call, Madam President."

"Tell them to go away," she snapped in frustration.

"It is the President of the United States."

Suddenly Sonja Petersen started to feel an overwhelming sense of dread. Jack Carter was one of the few who'd not called her with condolences upon the death of her father. Why now? She held out her hand. "Give me the phone."

After her aide was gone, she held the phone to her ear. "Mister President?"

"Madam President," came the terse reply.

"What can I do for you?"

"How about I cut through the crap and get straight to the point. Does that suit you, Sonja?"

"Please do, Jack."

"I have been getting some disturbing information about a planned genocide that is to take place on South African soil—"

"What information?" Sonja snapped, unable to help herself.

"Information that traces back to your government, Sonja. It's very disturbing."

"If you care to send me the intelligence that you have I shall have it investigated post haste. Could you elaborate some more?"

"Let's just say that it concerned your father and a known ISWA leader, Abadi Falomo."

"Are you accusing my father of consorting with a known terrorist, Jack? How preposterous."

"Come on, Sonja. We both know that it goes further than your father. And I shall warn you now, if whatever it is goes ahead, I shall bring crippling sanctions down upon your country so hard that your rand won't even be worth the paper it's printed on. I'll let the press have the intelligence that we have and let them run with it. Do you understand me?"

"All I understand is that I'm talking to a babbling old man who does not understand what he's saying and is messing in another county's sovereign affairs."

"Don't test me, Sonja."

"And don't you test me, Jack. I am stronger that you think."

Sonja hung up the phone and turned her hot gaze on Turner. "The Americans know. Which means it was probably them who tried to kidnap my father. You need to move the cocaine tomorrow."

"What about tonight?" Turner asked.

"Tonight, I want you to send a team of your men to an address on the city limits. There you will find a large warehouse. Have them kill everyone they find inside."

"What is the place?"

"It is a CIA safe house."

Turner was taken aback by the revelation. "You sure you want to do something like this, ma'am?"

"They are spies operating illegally on South African soil and will be treated as such. If the Americans want to make something of it, they can explain why they are in my country. After your men take care of that, you will return to the estate in Wits and be ready to load the cocaine in the morning."

"Where do you want us to take it?"

"Where it is meant to go. Soweto."

**Witwatersrand, South Africa**

The night was dark. Not the complete blackness that goes hand in hand with no moon but close enough to it. All three of the Team Reaper operators wore black biohazard suits and body armor as they approached the perimeter fence. The lights were on in the mansion even though Sonja Petersen wasn't there. They were each armed with their SIG Sauer M17s and suppressed an M4A1 SOPMOD or Special Operations Peculiar Modification. Ballistic helmets adorned their heads and NVGs pulled down over goggles showed them the way through the darkness.

Earlier, Swift had observed the arrival of a vehicle and the disembarkation of a man whom ISR later identified as Grady Turner. The boss of Roman Legion Security.

"I guess now is the time we find out if the fence is electrified," Cara said.

"It is," Kane said. "Do you have the tool?"

"I do."

"Use it."

Cara reached behind her and took out a foot-long piece of metal, just the thing to find out if the fence was indeed electrified.

"Hey, you know that if it is it'll light up like a Christmas tree, right?" Knocker told them.

"Slick couldn't find anything so it's likely not," Cara told the SAS man. "But if you want to grab it and find out, be my guest."

"Shit," Knocker growled and reached out with his hand. Before the other two could stop him, he'd grabbed the fence. "Happy now?"

"You're one crazy asshole, Knocker," Cara growled. "What if it had been live? You know nine out of ten are, right?"

"Then I'd be on my back and you'd be kissing me trying to get my ticker going," he shot back at her with a smile.

"Dick."

"Let's get this wire cut," Kane said quietly.

While Cara did that, he then called in. "Bravo Four, this is Reaper One, over."

"Good copy, Reaper One."

"We're about to breach the compound."

"Roger that. Just hold one while I finish a few things with their security system my end. Standby."

"Copy, standing by."

Cara finished the cutting of the wire and turned back to Kane. "We're in."

A couple of moments later Swift said, "Reaper One you're clear to breach the perimeter. The security feed is on a loop, but you still need to be in and out quickly."

"Roger that, Bravo Four. Out."

Kane looked at Cara. "Take us there, Two."

She slipped through the fence careful not to snag her suit in any way on the razor wire that might compromise it. She slipped across the open area towards a large hedge that surrounded a lavishly landscaped pool. Two men walked past the bushes where the three-person team held position until they had moved on. Cara skirted the pool with Kane and Knocker close behind her. From there they took the path down the left side of the mansion until the barn came into view.

Cara stopped and stood near the back wall. Kane used hand signals and the two of them separated while Knocker stayed at the rear of the large barn. They slid along the barn wall until they reached the front corner adjacent to the guards.

The two men stood either side of the large double doors oblivious to the danger they were in. Suddenly Swift's voice filled Kane's ear. "Hold, Reaper One. Danger close."

Kane froze and Cara could sense the tension in his stance. He waited patiently for the computer tech to elaborate. "You've got a roving patrol about to pass your position to the east."

Kane dropped to his knee and Cara followed suit. He raised his SOPMOD to his shoulder and held it ready. The shadow cast by the barn helped hide the team members while the two-man patrol walked past unaware of the trespassers.

"You're clear now, Reaper One," Swift said.

Kane didn't answer. He came to his feet and prepared to take out the guards. He felt Cara touch his shoulder, light pressure of her squeeze, and then he stepped out and around.

The two guards never knew what hit them. Kane squeezed the trigger on the SOPMOD twice, shifted his aim, and then did it again. Both Roman Legion contractors dropped where they stood.

Kane and Cara hurried forward and tried the barn door. It was unlocked so they grabbed the two dead men and dragged them through the narrow opening.

They dumped them on the floor and Kane called Knocker in. The three stood there looking around the interior at the scene before them. It was Knocker who said it. "Where the fuck are the drugs?"

Before them lay an empty floor with nothing visible. "Bravo Four, are you sure they put the drugs in this barn?"

"Affirmative, Reaper One."

"And they didn't take them out?"

"Negative."

Kane stared at the empty space before him through his NVGs. "Then we have a big problem."


"Check the floors," Kane whispered urgently and strode forward.

"What?" asked Knocker bemused. "In case you haven't realized mate there's nothing fucking here. It's only a matter of time before they see that their guards who were out front are AWOL."

"All the more reason for you to work faster, Knocker. Come on. Bravo Four, keep an eye out."

"Roger that."

The three team members started at the front of the barn and worked their way to the back but found nothing. It was all solid floor. "Go back over it," Kane snapped.

"We found nothing," Cara said.

"Do it. It's got to be there."

So, they started back over the straw-covered floor again and were halfway back along it when two things happened. They found the trapdoor which led down to the concealed basement, and their presence was discovered.

"Reaper One this is Bravo Four. You have two tangos approaching the barn."

"Good copy, Bravo four," Kane acknowledged. "Cara, we have two tangos inbound."

"Got it."

"So have I," Knocker said. "I've found the trapdoor."

Kane moved across to where the SAS man stood and started to help him scrape away the straw to reveal the large door in the floor, while Cara hurried toward the double doors at the front of the barn. She opened one side enough to see out of them. Two armed men were coming toward her. Suddenly they stopped and the man on the left took out a radio and began speaking into it.

"Reaper, we're compromised," she said softly into her comms.

"Deal with it, Cara."

"Roger that."

She raised the SOPMOD and sighted on the chest of the man with the radio. She fired twice and then switched her aim, taking down the second guard. "Two tangos down, Reaper. But you can expect more to be coming directly."

"Just give us time to get this done."

"Understood. Bravo Four call them out as you see them."

"Yes, ma'am."

The radio transmission stopped abruptly, and Grady Turner cursed loudly. They were here. How could he have let them get so close without knowing about it? "This is Turner," he said into his handset. "We have a security breach at the barn. Everybody, get over there now."

Turner hurried outside, taking with him an M6A2 as he went. He ran down the steps and across the gravel turnaround. Two other men joined him, and he could see an additional two jogging toward them. "We've got intruders at the Barn. They could be CIA or the ones who tried to take Paul Botha. We need to ensure they don't leave here alive."

When the barn came into sight the six of them slowed down to a walk, weapons at the ready. They approached cautiously and Turner waved two of his men forward. They still had ten meters to go when they saw their two men already down. Then a hailstorm of bullets ripped through the air and tore the two men apart.

"Make that six more, Reaper Two," Swift said in a low, expectant voice.

"I've got them, Bravo Four," Cara replied and waited until the two point men stumbled onto the two men already on the ground before she opened fire with devastating effect. The rate of fire that the SOPMOD put out ripped through the bodies of the two newcomers and they jerked wildly before falling to the ground damp from the evening dew. She shifted her aim to the additional four men behind the ones she'd just taken down and saw they'd dropped prone to the ground.

Bullets began to hammer into the thick wood doors. Some chewed splinters from the panels while others found soft patches and punched clean through. Cara dropped to her knee and began to return their fire.

"Reaper, you'd better hurry it up; the wolves are gathering."

"Just keep them back, Cara. We've located the drugs and all we need to do is plant the explosives."

"You forget one thing, Reaper. Once you plant the explosives we still need to get out of here."

"What's your point?"

"Reaper One, you may have a worsening situation on your hands," Swift said over the comms.

"What's that?"

"You seem to have gotten yourself sur-rounded."

"That's my point," Cara finally said.

A wild flurry of bullets slammed into the barn from all sides and forced Cara to lay flat. "Fuck me!" she hissed as she felt the displaced air from a misshapen round as it tumbled past. She flicked her fire selector around to auto and emptied her magazine at the shooters she could see.

"Son of a freaking bitch," Cara growled as she rolled onto her back and reloaded the weapon with a fresh thirty-round magazine. She rolled back over and fired off another long burst as more bullets hammered into the barn, splintering wood planks on the side of it.

"All right, we're done here, Cara," Kane said through the comms and both he and Knocker appeared, crawling along on their bellies from the top of the basement stairs. "How's it look out there?"

"How do you think?" she growled in response as a plank was shattered from multiple rounds.

"Slick, we need a way out of here," Kane said.

"It's not looking good. Reaper One. I'll do what I can."

"You've got three minutes," Kane told him.

"And then what? Or should I not ask?"

"Then we all die a fiery death."

"I knew I shouldn't have asked. Standby."

"Not for too long, mind," Kane replied.

A few seconds later Swift came back. "The only way I see is out the back."

Knocker glanced over his shoulder. "There's no fucking door there, mate. Do we walk through walls?"

"You can always go out the front," Swift said with a hint of mirth.

"How many are out there?" the SAS man asked.

"Three. At twelve, ten, and two."

"Roger that."

"Good luck."

Knocker rolled and checked his magazine. Then with a grunt, said, "Fuck it," and came to his feet, running at the rear wall like a runaway train.

When he hit the boards with his right shoulder the jarring impact rattled every part of the SAS man including his teeth. The wood splintered with a loud crack and Knocker felt the wall give and splinter as he crashed through. He hit the ground on the other side and rolled, came upon his knee, and took out the first shooter at two o'clock. There was no hesitation in him as he fired two more shots at the man who stood twelve, and then the one at ten. "Frigging assholes," he growled with a hint of disgust.

There was movement behind him as at first, Cara, and then Kane filled the void where the SAS man had punched through the barn wall.

A burst of gunfire ripped through the night from their right. All three operators swung to meet the deadly challenge. Through the green haze of their NVGs they picked out a shooter near a round shrub close by the house. All three fired at once and the security man fell back and lay still.

"OK, let's get moving," Kane said.

The three of them started to make toward

the perimeter fence where they originally cut the wire to get inside the grounds. Bullets from another shooter chased after them. Knocker stopped and turned. He fired a burst from the SOPMOD and then kept moving.

Behind them a sudden flash was met with a fiery eruption as the explosives detonated, incinerating every last bit of the packed cocaine as well as the anthrax it was laced with. Kane's NVGs flared and he was forced to lift them when he glanced back at the Norse pyre. Also illuminated were the remaining figures of the Roman Legion Security contractors who milled about in confusion, weapons silent. The Team Reaper commander turned back to follow the others as they continued towards the fence.

The explosion stunned them all. One moment the security men were exchanging fire with the intruders and the next night was torn apart by the detonation of the explosives. Turner cursed out loud as he realized what they had done. It was obvious that they, whoever they were, had known about the cocaine, which meant Botha had talked before he died.

"Fuck it!" Turner exploded as he understood it was all over. The plans of Sonja Petersen had just gone up with the barn and she would hold him personally responsible. The only way out he could see was if the other team took out the CIA safe house. Maybe then there might be some forgiveness in the harsh exterior of the unforgiving woman. But he doubted it.

# CHAPTER 18

*CIA Safehouse, Johannesburg*

"The team is offsite, Luis, and on their way back here," Swift told Ferrero. "Mission accomplished."

"I'll let the general know," the operations commander said. "Then we can get out of Dodge and that will be that."

"Not quite, I'm afraid," Sacks reported as he appeared beside them. "It would seem we're about to have visitors."

"Hostile?" Ferrero asked.

"More than likely. Three black SUVs traveling fast just tripped our early warning system one klick out."

Ferrero took his M17 from his hip holster and checked it. Swift did the same. Sacks said, "See Mertens, he'll set you up with a vest and a heavier weapons selection if you want one."

"What's the plan?" Ferrero asked.

"We have a scorched earth policy. We hold them until the last moment and then leave. That'll give the techs time to get rid of what they need to."

"Just tell us what to do."

"Shoot straight."


There were eight men from Roman Legion. Every one of them was heavily armed and moved with all the skill of trained military personnel. They weren't, however, expecting the reception they received, expecting that their attack under the cover of darkness would give them the element of surprise.

Except the surprise was on them, and the shooters began to die as soon as they stepped from their vehicles. Immediately two fell under a hail of lead that punched holes not only in flesh but almost every exposed quarter panel of the SUVs. Ferrero picked out a security man with his SOPMOD that Ryan Mertens had supplied him with. The bad guy's legs kicked out from beneath him and he shouted in pain.

Soddenly one of the vehicles exploded with a loud crump and a flash of orange lit the darkness. The remaining shooters scattered for better cover.

"Luis!" Sacks called over. "There's more coming in!"

A roar of engines and flash of headlights signaled the arrival of an additional two SUVs. Six more shooters clambered out and joined the fight. Beside Ferrero, Swift sprayed bullets at the new arrivals like some kind of maniac possessed. "Hey," Ferrero shouted at him. "Pick your targets."

"I am. It's the only way I can hit anything."

"Shit a fucking brick."

"Changing!" Swift shouted like he actually knew what he was doing before fumbling with a fresh magazine. He held it up and looked at Ferrero. "How do I do this?"

Shaking his head, Ferrero took the SOP-MOD and changed out the magazine. As he handed it back, he said, "Remind me to get Cara to give you time on the range."

Swift put it back up to his shoulder and squeezed the trigger, expecting a sustained burst to spew forward. Instead it fired one shot. He looked back at his boss and called across to him. "Something's wrong."

"Just keep pulling the damned trigger."

The tech did and the weapon fired again. "Hey what did you do to it?"

"Just shut up and shoot."

Suddenly Ryan Mertens appeared beside them. "They're done inside. It's time for us to leave."

Ferrero nodded. "Slick, we're going!"

"We're getting on top of them," the tech called back.

"Come on, Rambo, before you turn bullet-proof."

All of the CIA shooters fell back into the building. Ferrero and Swift followed Mertens down a flight of stairs to the basement where they found an old steel door wide open and Sacks waiting for them. "I see you're still with us. Move along the tunnel and up the ladder when you reach it. There'll be vehicles there to take us to the consulate. I'll see you there."

"You're not coming?" Ferrero asked.

"I'll be along directly."

The Team Reaper operations commander led Swift along the tunnel. As they went, he called back over his shoulder. "Get in touch with Reaper and the others when we get above ground. Tell them to abort their current mission and regroup on us at the consulate."

The ladder was metal, rusted from its years below ground. When they broke the surface, true to Sacks' word there were SUVs waiting. The first one was taking off as they ran towards them. The second and third were still waiting with their drivers. They climbed into the back of the one in front and as the driver put his foot on the gas, Swift made the call to reroute Kane and the others to the consulate.

### Camp Lemonnier, Djibouti

"Ma'am, we have news," Brooke Reynolds told Thurston who was looking over new intel supplied by the CIA.

She looked up. "What is it?"

"The team was able to neutralize the threat, ma'am, but before they got back the private contractors that President Petersen employs hit the CIA safehouse and they were forced to evacuate."

"Is everyone all right?"

"Yes, ma'am, they are all at the consulate in Johannesburg."

"That's something, I guess. At least they're safe."

Reynolds winced. "Not exactly true, General."

"Why?"

"It seems the president wasn't too happy about the team taking out her stash of cocaine. She's had them declared terrorists, and aggressors to her country who attacked her home in the hope of her assassination. The American consulate is currently surrounded by South African armed forces and she's demanding that the ones responsible be handed over immediately."

"Good grief. Is she fucking serious?"

"I'm afraid so. Ma'am."

"Who's handling it?"

"Ambassador Blummentritt."

"Shit, get me on a plane now. And someone get me Hank Jones."

"What can you tell me about Johannesburg, Mary?" Hank Jones asked via the video call.

"I probably know as much as you, sir. The team did accomplish their mission and then the private contractors attacked the CIA safe house."

The general nodded. "The crazy damned woman is calling it an act of war, an assassination attempt by terrorists, and all kinds of crap. She's refusing to call off her troops until they are turned over. Hell, the people have started burning the American flag in the street because it was conveniently leaked that they are American."

"I'm headed down there, sir."

"Be careful, Mary. And let the ambassador handle it."

"Sir, the ambassador can't handle shit. Don't be surprised if the asshole hands them over just to save his own hide. Can you get the president to give me authority to deal with this when I get onsite?"

"I don't know, Mary. It'll mean treading on a few toes—"

"Sorry, General, but I don't give a fuck whose toes I tread on. They're my people, I'll get them out."

"I'll see what I can do."

"Thank you, sir."

"Good luck."

Thurston's voice was icy when she said, "It'll be that bitch who'll need the luck, Hank. She's about to learn that committing genocide is political suicide."

### Mexico City, Mexico

The white Jeep eased to a stop outside a large nightclub and Flavia Ojeda turned the engine off. The three occupants sat there and waited a moment as the early morning sun beat down and warmed the interior. All three of them were dressed in jeans and loose-fitting shirts which could be pulled down to hide the hand-guns that each carried.

"You sure this guy isn't going to shoot you

on sight, amigo?" Arenas asked.

"He very well could," Traynor acknowledged the problem that might arise. "But I'm hoping he's the forgiving type."

"You're a crazy son of a bitch, you know that?"

Traynor glanced across at Ojeda and winked at her. "Only get one shot at life. Might as well make the most of it."

She smiled at him. "Let's go and see if yours ends here."

They climbed from the Jeep and walked across the sidewalk and up the three steps leading to the front door of the nightclub. Arenas was the first there and tried the door, half expecting it to be locked due to the early hour. With a tug the door swung open and they all passed through into the dimly lit interior.

The inside smelled of cheap perfume, cigarillo smoke, and stale alcohol. Not to mention puke. There were four men and three scantily clad women – no two scantily clad women; the third was completely naked and was straddled across one of the men, riding him with reckless abandon atop the pool table in the far corner. "Someone's having fun," Ferrero said as her cries grew louder as she neared orgasm.

"Do you see your man?" Ojeda asked.

"Nope."

One of the Mexicans saw them standing there. He reached under his jacket and both Arenas and Traynor tensed. "What the fuck do you want?" the man asked. "We're closed. Get out."

"I'm here to see Messinas," Traynor said.

"He's –"

Suddenly the woman's cries of passion reached fever pitch and drowned out the Mexican's words. He turned to the two who were still humping and shouted, "Will you shut the fuck up!"

They quietened down but never stopped.

The Mexican turned his attention back to the three newcomers. So too the other two. He wiped his hands casually down the front of his suit coat and said, "Carlo is busy."

"He'll want to see me," Traynor said.

The man shook his head slowly and wiped at his suit coat once more but this time he left his hands halfway down the lapel. "No. I said he's busy, gringo. Come back maybe never."

Traynor nodded slowly then spoke clearly so his words would be understood. "If you've got a weapon in a shoulder holster under that coat of yours, and I'm guessing you have, you might want to consider not pulling it. If you do, you'll be dead before you get halfway. All I want is to talk to Messinas about a shipment of cocaine that Amaya Caro brought into the country along with a known terrorist."

There was uncertainty in the man's eyes as he contemplated what he'd just been told. His two friends stepped forward to stand at either shoulder. The silence in the room suddenly became heavy. The pair on the pool table had stopped screwing and were also looking in the direction of the newcomers. Even the two women who'd been standing near the bar.

"Are you going to get him or not?"

The Mexican looked at the man to his right. "Do it."

"See, we can all be friends here."

The man instructed to fetch Messinas disappeared and then returned a few minutes later. Not far behind him came a tall man dressed in a white suit with neatly trimmed facial hair. He took one look at Traynor and said, "Tell me why I shouldn't kill you right now, puta."

"Because you're my friend?" Traynor asked.

The cartel man nodded at his man who had spoken to them when they'd entered.

Traynor tried again. "Or maybe because if your people try anything my friends will put a bullet in your head and then kill everyone else."

Messinas stared at Traynor's face looking for a bluff but couldn't see one. He held up his hand and asked, "What is it you want, Traynor?"

"Amaya Caro brought in a shipment of cocaine just recently. I want to know about it."

"Why should I tell you what Amaya does?"

"If it works out for you then maybe your boss will be gone, and you might get your father's business back."

That got his attention. "Do you still work for the DEA?"

Traynor shook his head. "I work for people who are much worse."

The cartel man cocked a disbelieving eyebrow. "Worse?"

"Uh-huh."

"How much worse could it be?"

"Mendoza, El Conglomerado, that kind of worse."

"That was you?"

"That was the people I work for."

"And you think you can get Amaya Caro."

"Already had one go at her."

"And now you want my help?" Messinas asked.

"Your boss has smuggled some bad cocaine in along with a man called Abadi Falomo. ISWA terrorist. He's trying to get the cocaine into the US," Traynor explained.

"Why should that concern me?"

"Because if that cocaine gets into the US it could kill thousands. And if that happens, my government will blame the cartels. It won't matter which one, they will come after all of them. They will declare war on them all and deploy soldiers across the border in an effort to clean out every last one."

"They would not dare. The Mexican government wouldn't stand for it," Messinas declared.

"Do you think they would give a fuck what your government thinks. Amaya Caro will have aided and abetted in a terrorist attack. They'll come and they'll roll right over whoever stands in their way."

Now came the uncertainty. Messinas glanced at Ojeda and then at Arenas before coming back to Ojeda. "I know you. You would help these people?"

"Only to stop what would happen if that bitch isn't stopped doing this," the Mexican intelligence officer said. "But you can stop both her and the American."

Messinas nodded. "OK."

"Where are they?" Traynor asked.

"Ciudad Juarez."

"What are they doing there?"

"That is where the cocaine is going across the border."

"How?" Traynor snapped urgently. "How

are they getting it across?"

"The tunnels."

"Damn it, Messinas, what tunnels?"

"At the warehouse."

"Give me an address so we can get there."

Messinas shook his head. "It is too late. The cocaine has already gone across."

"Damn it," Traynor cursed. "Where the hell is it going?"

"I don't know. But Amaya will know."

"Then we're back at the question, where is she? If the cocaine has gone across then she's not going to be in Juarez."

Messinas gave him a funny look and the former DEA undercover knew immediately that he'd been stalling for time. "You fucking son of a bitch," Traynor growled and reached for his weapon. Arenas and Ojeda did the same. Quicker than spit everyone in the room had their weapons out, pointed in all directions.

"Put the gun down, amigo," Messinas gloated. "We are done here."

"The hell we are. You put yours down."

"I think that it might be easier if you did as you were told," a new voice was added to the conversation.

Traynor glanced at the new arrivals and instantly knew who they both were. Amaya Caro and The American. Arenas asked, "You want me to shoot him, Pete?"

"In a minute, Carlos."

"No, I will do it," Ojeda snapped and Traynor nodded.

"He is the one?"

"He is the one who owes me a life."

"Then he's all yours," he told her. Then, "Where's Falomo taking the cocaine, Amaya?"

"What does it matter?" she asked nonchalantly.

"It matters. It's laced with fucking anthrax."

"Why should that worry me?"

"I think we kill her too, amigo," Arenas said. "Then we just find the drugs and the terrorist and kill him."

"You're a mite keen to die, my Mexican friend," Franks stated.

"You think we come here alone?" Arenas asked him. "Why would we come into the nest of La Vibora without someone to watch our backs?"

"You're bluffing," Franks said with an assured smile.

"You shut up," Traynor growled at him. "You're a fucking dead man whichever way this ends."

"You ever been stung by an Escorpiones, gringo?"

"What?"

Suddenly the room erupted in violence as Domingo Cruz and his men burst in. Flash-bangs were deployed and then gunfire ripped the place apart. Cartel men jerked wildly as automatic fire punched into them. The girls dived for the floor as around them men started to die. Ojeda shifted her aim and centered her weapon on Franks who was already moving and reaching for his own weapon. But even though he'd been military trained he was still taken by surprise, and before he could get his handgun out, two bullets slammed into his chest.

But the intelligence officer wasn't done just yet. Ignoring all of the gunfire around her she stepped forward and pumped another three shots into the Amaya Caro's hired killer. He jerked once more and then lay still as death overcame him.

A sense of satisfaction settled over Ojeda when she saw The American die. At last her husband was avenged. At last –

A hammer blow hit her in her chest and propelled her backward. The air rushed from Ojeda's lungs as she tried to comprehend what had just happened. She gathered her feet under herself and looked up to see Amaya Caro's snarling face in front of her. In her hand she still had her personal weapon pointed at Ojeda.

The intelligence officer gasped for air and eventually it came. Her lungs filled and relief flooded her. But there was still the cartel bitch to deal with.

Amaya Caro suddenly realized that something was wrong. Ojeda wasn't dying, she was gaining strength for the bullet hadn't passed through the vest she wore under her coat. She snapped off another shot but, in her haste forgot to aim. However, Ojeda wasn't going to make the same mistake. She squeezed the trigger three times and was rewarded each time by the convulsion of a bullet impact as each round slammed home violently.

Amaya slumped to the floor in an untidy heap, her whited blouse stained with a deep red which seemed to spread rapidly. It was a good day.

To her left Traynor had dispatched Messinas with two shots. One to his chest and one to his face. The Mexican never stood a chance. Arenas had killed one of his men while the Scorpions had done for the rest. When the gunfire died the only noise to be heard was that of the women who worked in the club.

Traynor heard a groan and his head turned. He saw Ojeda down on one knee holding herself. He hurried across to her. "Are you OK?" he asked her.

"Took a round to the vest," she gasped. "That bitch shot me. But I got her."

The former DEA undercover stared at Amaya Caro. She lay unmoving in a large patch of blood. "Yes, you did."

He helped her to her feet. "Looks like you got The American too."

"He deserved to be killed," she growled. "They both did."

"No argument here," Traynor agreed. He sensed some movement beside him, and Cruz appeared. "Your men all right?"

The Mexican officer nodded. "Nothing major." He nodded at Amaya. "At last we are rid of La Vibora. And her hired killer."

Traynor nodded. "All we have to do now is find out where Falomo has taken the cocaine."

# CHAPTER 19

*United States Consulate, Johannesburg*

Soon after the sun had come up in the east under a sky of red, Ambassador Angus Blummentritt called the men before him. Once they had gathered in his office, he silently studied them as though seeing them for the first time. Ferrero became suspicious almost immediately. Kane, on the other hand, knew from the look in his eyes that the gutless son of a bitch was about to betray them all.

"I have decided," Blummentritt started, and then stopped as though he was reconsidering what he was about to say. Then, "I have decided that you shall all be handed over to the South African authorities to face their justice system."

"The fuck we are, Mate," Knocker blurted out. "You can go and screw yourself. You try anything like that, and I'll put a fucking bullet in your head."

Blummentritt looked aghast that someone would actually speak to him like that. He glanced at Ferrero as though looking for him to intervene. Instead, he said, "What he said."

"I beg your pardon?"

"He said fuck you," Kane answered.

The ambassador nodded. "I thought this might happen." He reached out across his polished wood desk and touched a button on his intercom. "Send them in."

The door burst open and a squad of marines burst in armed with automatic weapons. They stood with them pointed at the five men who were taken by surprise that one of their own could do something like this. "You won't get away with this," Ferrero said. "Hank Jones won't allow you to do it."

"It isn't up to Hank Jones. I get my orders from the State Department."

"Then they sure as shit won't let you do this," Ferrero growled.

"They will agree with whatever I do. This is my station and I'm in charge. The South African Government has sent a detail to take you into custody. We will not go to war with them because of a black ops assassination attempt."

"You stupid cock," Knocker chuckled. "Who

told you that bullshit story?"

"The evidence speaks for itself. You attacked the residence of the president. Not to mention killed her father."

"She was responsible for that, Blummentritt," Kane snapped. "Her and her new bodyguard."

"You were there, I've seen the footage from cameras."

"You are one dumb wanker, you know that?" Knocker said, shaking his head.

"Is this guy for real?" Swift asked.

"Don't worry, old mate," Knocker reassured him, "He's a little screwy in the old noggin."

The intercom buzzed and a voice said, "Mister Ambassador, they're here."

"Send them in."

The dark wood doors swung inward and five people entered the sparsely furnished office. The marines stepped aside, however kept their weapons on the five Team Reaper men. Blummentritt smiled warmly and said, "Madam President, these are the men you require."

Sonja Petersen gave him a mirthless smile. "Thank you. They will be tried for the murder of my father and the attempted assassination of myself."

"You could have sent someone for them instead of coming yourself."

She shook her head. "This I wanted to over-see in person."

Beside her, Grady Turner looked at Knocker and frowned. The SAS man nodded. "Yeah, it's me, you money-grabbing, murdering, prick."

"Knocker fucking Jensen," Turner rumbled. "This is turning into an even better day than I thought."

"Make the most of it, cock, it's going to be your last."

"Do we really have to listen to this?" Petersen asked.

Ferrero stared at Blummentritt. "Are you going to hand us over to a woman who's willing to commit genocide to serve her white power aspirations? Someone who is just itching to bring Apartheid back and killed her own father to keep her secret."

"It was your people who killed my father," Petersen stated.

"No, we didn't, you silly cow," Knocker snapped. "But we sure fucked up your plans though."

The South African president glared at the SAS man. "I'm sure that I don't know what you're talking about, you despicable little man. But I do know that I'm going to enjoy watching you be shot for the attempted assassination of a statesman."

Knocker grabbed at his crotch. "Assassinate this—"

"Enough!" Blummentritt screeched. "Get them out of here."

"I'd hold it right there if I was you," General Mary Thurston said loudly as she walked into the ambassador's office. "Those men are going nowhere."

A look of annoyance came over Blummentritt's face. "Who are you?"

"General Mary Thurston, head of The Worldwide Drug Initiative. And right now, your direct superior, you slimy little weasel."

"You most certainly are not," the ambassador snapped indignantly.

"If you have a problem with my authority then feel free to give President Carter a call. He's the one who gave me the authority."

"He wouldn't—"

"Sit down and shut up."

Blummentritt opened his mouth to continue the debate but Thurston's hot scowl shut it and he sat down. The General turned to her people. "Are you lot all right?"

"We are now," Ferrero replied.

"What is the meaning of this?" Petersen demanded. She stepped forward, closer to the woman who dared challenge her authority. "These assassins are in my custody."

"In case you haven't realized yet, you're still on US sovereign soil. These are my men and therefore they belong to me. You cannot have them."

"I beg to differ," the South African president shot back.

"Marines! Contact front!" Thurston barked.

Each marine in the room brought up their weapons and pointed them at Petersen and her entourage. "What is the meaning of this?" she demanded.

"This is you leaving one way or the other, Madam President," Thurston said. "And by the way, you can expect a visit from the UN any day now, who will be inquiring about your dealings with a wanted terrorist, putting anthrax in cocaine you planned to distribute throughout Soweto, and the murder of your own father."

"How absurd."

"We've sent all the evidence to The Hague. You'll face a whole lot of trouble, not to mention the shit coming down from your own people."

"Prove it."

"Like I said, we've everything we need. Now, I'm going to take my people out of here later today. If there is any problem, I'll know where to come looking and finish the so-called assassination. If I was you, I'd resign and leave the country before the ANC get hold of you."

"You have nothing," Petersen hissed.

"Try me."

Without another word the South African president, whirled and stormed from the ambassador's office with her bodyguards following.

"I guess that told her," Kane said.

"Stuck up bitch," Thurston grumbled.

"I intend to lodge a formal protest with my office," Blummentritt snarled, trying to get his courage back. "You haven't heard the end of this."

"The offer to call the president is still there, Ambassador. Have at it."

"I think the weasel is right about one thing," Ferrero said after they left the office.

"What's that?"

"I think Sonja Petersen hasn't finished with us yet."

"Let the bitch come," Thurston said. "We'll be ready for her."

Thurston disconnected the call and turned to the others. "That's one less headache for us but it gives us a new one."

"News ma'am?" Kane asked.

"Amaya Caro and The American are dead. They tried to ambush our people in a nightclub in Mexico City. But Traynor had set up a surprise of his own just in case. Caro and her man kind of fell into their laps."

"Any word on Falomo?" Ferrero asked.

"Nothing. I need to ring the general and let him know that the son of a bitch is in the country. We're all headed to El Paso later today. The others have already left."

"How are we going to do that?" Kane asked. "Swift has been keeping an eye on our surrounds and they're out there waiting."

"Who is?"

"Roman Legion. The troops have been withdrawn but not the contractors."

Knocker snorted. "Let's just walk out there and go toe-to-toe with them assholes. Get it over and done with."

"It might just come to that," Kane allowed.

Thurston nodded in agreement. "That bitch has let them off the leash. Gear up. We leave within the hour."

"Just hold up a little there, General," Knocker said. "If we can delay our departure until after dark, we might be able to work something out."

"Such as?"

Knocker turned to Swift. "How many of

them bastards out there?"

"I counted three SUVs."

"Give me an hour after dark, ma'am and I'll have them all decommissioned, and we can just drive out of the gates."

Thurston considered the option the SAS man laid out before her and then nodded. "OK, do it."

"I'm going to need a shitload of bullets to make up some improvised explosives."

"Anything you need just requisition it."

"Yes, ma'am."


Knocker slid under the first SUV like a snake under a doorway. Quiet and without any fuss he placed the first of his explosives near the rear axle. He waited a moment before he slid back out and slunk toward a dark blind spot where Kane was waiting for him.

"Piece of piss," he said with a smile. "I reckon them pricks were asleep."

"Two more to go," Kane said.

"If they are like the first then it should be a walk in the park."

Keeping to the shadows they moved across two streets to where the second vehicle was stationed. Like the first, Knocker had little trouble about placing the explosives. The third, however was a different story. And it all came down to an empty can of soda.

Knocker had just slid under the final SUV when he hit the empty can with his left hand. It rattled across the asphalt with what seemed to be an unbelievably loud noise. Knocker cursed silently and heard the voices in the vehicle right before the door opened.

The SAS man reached down to his thigh, forgetting about the explosives. His fingers touched the butt of the M17 in its holster. His hand wrapped around it and he eased the weapon from the holster. Knocker saw the boots hit the street and then he saw the legs bend as the person started to crouch down.

The M17 came up pointed in the man's direction. Knocker hoped Kane was watching this. The head appeared and the man's face came into focus. The handgun bucked in Knocker's fist and the man's head snapped back as the bullet smashed into it.

The vehicle rocked as its other occupants tumbled from it. Knocker heard Kane's gun fire twice and another man fell beside the SUV. The SAS operative scrambled from beneath the vehicle and came up into a firing position, searching for another target. But Kane beat him to it and the third contractor fell dead in the street.

"You OK?" Kane called over to Knocker.

"That's fucking bollocks that is. Now they'll all know something's up. Call your boss lady, Reaper. Get us all out of here."

Kane didn't have to. As soon as the gunfire started, she ordered the two SUVs they were using out the gate. The lead one stopped beside them, and the two men climbed in. "Blow the damned vehicles," Thurston snapped.

With the press of a button the two primed homemade explosives detonated with orange flashes. Small mushroom clouds shot skyward as the vehicles sped off down the street away from the consulate.

"Where are we headed?" Kane asked the general.

"There's a small airfield outside of Johannesburg. We'll leave from there. A plane will take us to Nairobi. From there we fly to El Paso."

"What about Petersen and Grady Turner?" Knocker asked.

"The UN and her own people will deal with Sonja Petersen. As for Turner, karma always finds a way."

"And me?" Knocker asked.

"You ever been to the States?" Thurston asked.

"Once."

"Make it twice. I'll buy you a big old Texas

steak to say thanks for your help."

"You got yourself a deal, General, but you'd better make it after we get Falomo."

"Let's do that then."

"You buying one for the rest of us, General?" Kane asked.

"You buy your own. I only shout our visitors."

"Yes, ma'am."

### El Paso, Texas

Once word went out about a terror threat, the city was in lockdown. There was virtually nowhere for Falomo to go to escape the city with the shipment of cocaine. Not that it mattered, he would find another way to distribute it. But first he had to make sure it was still secure.

Pickford and Sons Trucking Company on the north side of El Paso had a large freight yard with many shipping containers stacked throughout. The Ford pickup approached the main gates and slowed down. The boom stayed down, and the pickup was forced to stop. From a small hut the security guard emerged, a flashlight in his hand. He shone it into the interior of the Ford and illuminated both driver and passenger. "Chet? What are you doing back here?"

Chet Booker looked sheepishly at the security guard. "I left something here that I needed to take home with me."

"Yeah? Like what?"

"You know my girl, Renae, right Clem?"

Clem the guard nodded. "Uh-huh."

"Well I finally got up the courage to ask her to marry me and—"

"Congratulations," Clem blurted out before Chet could finish.

"Yeah well it would be that if I hadn't forgot the damned ring. I left it in my locker."

"Oh," the guard said. "That was a little mistake right there."

"Not wrong. I just need to go get it and I'll be gone."

Clem nodded. "Sure. Who's your friend?"

"That's Renae's brother. Wally."

Chet could have shot himself right there and then at the glaring mistake he'd just made. Clem leaned in close and said in a low voice, "He's black."

Chet sensed Falomo tense beside him and knew that the terrorist had his right hand wrapped around the butt of a Glock handgun. He said, "He's adopted, you ass."

The guard smiled and stepped back. He shook his head and said, "I'll get the gate for you."

He stepped back inside and pressed the button which raised the boom gate. Chet eased the pickup forward and breathed a sigh of relief.

He took the truck through the gate and along the driveway until he came across a left turn. He took it and instead of pulling into the lot, he kept driving until he reached a small crossroads and turned right. He drove between a couple of container stacks and then took the next right again before stopping halfway along. He looked across at Falomo and said, "This is it."

They climbed from the truck and stood in front of the container. "Are you sure?" the terrorist asked.

"Yes. I put it here myself."

"Open it."

Chet reached into the back of his truck and took out some cutters. He then cut the lock and the shipping seal and opened the first door.

"I can't see anything," Falomo said.

"Just hold on a minute," Chet said and walked back to the truck again. He reached under the driver's seat and took out a flashlight. He switched it on and shone it inside the container at a wall of boxes. Chet started to take a section of the front row out. Before long the hole was big enough and he started on the second and then the third.

Behind the third was a compartment with a door. Chet opened it and stepped aside, passing the flashlight to Falomo.

The terrorist stepped into the container and walked through the door. Beyond the opening was the pallet that had made its way from Africa by air to Mexico and then been concealed inside the container and transported across the border. Now it was hidden here at the transport yard, awaiting distribution.

"Is it all good?" Chet asked.

"It is," Falomo replied with his deep African accent.

"Hey, what are you doing here, Chet?"

Chet's heart sank as he turned and saw Clem standing there with his flashlight.

"What are you doing in that container? You know you can't go opening them."

Chet stepped to one side and said in a would you believe tone, "Looking for my ring."

The sound of a suppressed handgun slapped from within the container and two rounds hammered into the security man's chest. He staggered a little and looked down shining the flashlight on the front of his shirt. Twin red patches had already started to spread. He looked up at Chet, confusion on his face.

Another shot sounded and Clem collapsed at the opening of the container.

"Fuck it," Chet swore.

"We have to move the cocaine," Falomo stated.

"No fucking shit. And there's only one place we can take it. I have a basement we can keep it in until everything quietens down."

"That will do. Then we will distribute it."

"Are you crazy?" Chet asked. "The whole city is crawling with law enforcement. We'll be lucky to make it to my place without getting pulled over."

"Load it, now," Falomo demanded and pointed his weapon at Chet.

"All right, all right, hold onto your horses."

Twenty minutes of hard toil saw the truck bed loaded with the cocaine. "There. All we have to do now is get it out of here."

They climbed into the pickup after covering the load with a tarpaulin. Chet turned it and headed back the way they'd come. At the front gate they were met by a second security guard. He walked around the front of the truck to Chet's side and said, "Did you see Clem around, Chet?"

Chet shook his head. "Nope. No sign of him, Roy."

The man frowned. "I wonder where he got to. OK. I'll open the gate and let you out."

A wave of relief swept over Chet, aware that

Falomo still had the Glock waiting, ready in case of trouble.

Suddenly Roy stopped and turned. He frowned and looked at the truck. "What's under the tarpaulin, Chet?"

"Not much."

"You'd better show me."

"Aww, come on, Roy. Let me go home."

"Sorry, Chet. Rules are rules. Even for those who work here."

Chet sighed; he knew what was coming next. He climbed from the truck and walked to the back. Roy was concentrating on what he was doing that he never realized that Falomo had stepped out of the vehicle as well.

The cover swept back and at the same time the terrorist shot Roy in the back of his head. Chet looked down at the dead man and shook his head. "Shit."

He reached down and grabbed Roy by the collar. He dragged him towards the guard hut and dumped him on the floor. Then he hit the switch and the boom gate rose into the air.

Chet hurried back out to the truck and climbed in. He threw it into gear and put his foot on the gas. The Ford shot forward and it roared off into the night.

### Worldwide Drug Initiative HQ, El Paso

"What have you got?" Thurston asked Swift upon being summoned to his workstation.

"Last night two security guards were killed at the Pickford and Sons trucking yard," he explained. "The call came in before midnight to the El Paso PD. From what I can gather whoever did it, was after something hidden in one of the containers there. It seems one of the firm's security people sprung them in the act and they killed him."

"Security footage?"

"Plenty of that, just not in the right areas."

"What about at the main gate?"

"Not working. They lodged a repair order yesterday afternoon."

"We need to get some people out there to look around. Send Cara and—"

"I'll go."

Thurston turned and looked at Knocker. "How long have you been standing there?"

"Long enough."

She shook her head. "No. You stay where I can keep an eye on you."

"Come on, General, what trouble can I get into with Cara looking over my shoulder?"

"No."

"You brought me all the way to America just to keep me locked up inside these walls? Listen, I won't get into trouble unless I ask first. Besides, I've had some experience with this biological shit."

Thurston sighed. "All right then. But if you put one foot out of line, I'll tell Cara to shoot it off. Understood?"

"Yes, ma'am."

"And let her ask the questions. She used to be a deputy sheriff."

"Yes, ma'am."

"Go find her and tell her I want to see her."

"Yes, ma'am."

Ten minutes later Cara was there. "You wanted me, General?"

Thurstone nodded. "Yes. I need you to head over to a place called Pickford and Sons Trucking Company. There was an incident there last night and I want you to ask questions about it."

"You think it could be tied up with our cocaine shipment?"

"It could be. Get over there and find out. Go armed and take your government ID. It should give you all the access you need. If not, I'll give Hank Jones a heads up and you can call him. Any questions?"

"No."

"Good luck. I hope you find something."

They started to walk out of Thurston's office when she said, "If Knocker gives you any problems, just shoot him."

"Already had that thought, General."

"Good."

### Pickford and Sons Trucking Company, El Paso

The SUV eased to a stop at the curb and the pair of them climbed out. They walked towards the police tape at the boom gate and were stopped by a uniformed officer. "Can I help you at all?" was his greeting.

Cara took out her ID and said, "We'd like to speak to the detective in charge."

The officer frowned. "Ain't never heard of no Worldwide Drug company."

Cara let his ignorance slide. "I can't help that."

"I can't let you through."

"Just get the lead detective so I can ask him some questions."

"I don't know, he's pretty busy," the officer whined.

"Listen…what's your name?"

"Earl."

"Listen, Earl, we're trying to stop a potential terrorist attack, OK? And we need to speak to the lead detective."

"I don't—"

"For fuck sake, you bloody tosser, get the man in charge before I take your badge off you and jamb it up your ass sideways," Knocker growled in a low voice. "If this terrorist prick we're chasing does some bad shit you'll be the knob they blame."

Taken aback by the vehemence of Knocker's words, the officer's mouth worked open and closed. Then he reached for the walkie handpiece and talked into it. "This is the gate. Tell Detective Mallory that he's needed down here yesterday."

Two minutes later a tall, thin man appeared wearing a creased suit and a less than happy expression. "Who wants me?" he growled in a tired manner.

Cara introduced herself and Knocker then showed him her credentials. "We would like to get a look at your crime scene and ask you a few questions if that's OK?"

The middle-aged detective had dealt with enough government institutions to know that when they asked, they weren't really asking. He lifted the tape. "Follow me."

Once inside the cordon the detective asked, "What do you want to know?"

"Do you have any footage of what happened?"

"Not much. We have a vehicle and not much more. The cameras at the gate were conveniently out of action."

"Would you mind if we saw it?"

Mallory shrugged. "Sure."

He took them over to the guard hut and they went inside. "Just watch your step."

They stepped around evidence techs as they gathered all they could to help with the case. Then over at the desk Mallory set a feed running on a computer. They watched as it switched from one feed to another, every now and then the screen went blank as it came across a camera that wasn't working.

"That's it," the detective sighed.

"Do you have any idea who was in the pickup?" Cara asked.

"We're running through employees at the moment. We figure that to get here they needed to be either an employee or have a legitimate pass. My bet is that they worked here."

"Makes sense," Cara agreed. She reached into her pocket and took out her cell. She hit speed dial and said, "Slick, can you run a deep background check on all of the employees here at the trucking company?"

She waited for his answer and then said, "Thanks," before hanging up. "Sometimes things get done quicker outside of channels," she said to Mallory.

"You ex-PD?"

"Sheriff's deputy."

The detective nodded. "I'd appreciate if you could share anything you find."

"Sure. I don't see a problem."

Mallory thought he'd test the relationship. "So, what's your interest in this?"

"We're looking for Abadi Falomo."

"I heard of him. He's our number one wanted at the moment. You figure he's got something to do with this?"

Cara said, "That's what we want to find out. We were in Africa trying to find a shipment of cocaine and some captives which ISWA had. It turns out that Falomo has laced the coke with anthrax."

"Motherfucker," Marlow grunted. "If he gets that distributed then people will drop like flies. Junkies come in all shapes and sizes. You'd better come look at the container."

Their next stop was the container. They looked around inside and then came back out. "It's obvious that there was something in here."

Mallory nodded. "Our techs went over it and initial results are that there was cocaine in here. The question is was it the same stuff you're looking for?"

"I think we might be onto something,"

Knocker said, holding up a small piece of what looked to be some kind of flora. "Turraeanthus Africana."

Cara rolled her eyes. "English, Knocker. Use your native tongue."

"African White Mahogany. Native to Nigeria."

"I guess that answers our question. I'll let the general know. You have a BOLO out on that truck, Detective?"

"I sure do but now we know what we're faced with I think I'd better inform my captain."

# CHAPTER 20

**Worldwide Drug Initiative HQ, El Paso**

"I think I have something, ma'am," Swift called across to Thurston as she stood watching the security feed over and over.

"I'm glad you were able to find something; I'm starting to go cross-eyed."

She walked across to where he sat, and he looked up at her. "I was able to find the vehicle by searching security and traffic cams within a two-mile radius. The pickup belongs to a Chet Booker. When I looked into him a little further, he came up with a record as long as your arm. His latest was a stint in the pokey for drug possession. The police tried to get him on a trafficking charge, but his lawyer got him off. Guess who he's tied to."

"Amaya Caro?" Thurston asked.

"The Paso Vipers, which has ties to Caro's cartel."

"Not anymore they don't," Thurston said. "But you can bet your last dollar someone is already thinking of filling the void. Do you have an address for him?"

"Already sent it to Cara and to Knocker. They should be mobile shortly."

"All right. Get their comms up and we'll follow their progress. Get what you can on the big screen. Hopefully we'll find something. I'll get Luis—"

"I'm already here, Mary."

She turned and saw Ferrero walking towards her. "It looks as though I'm becoming redundant," Thurston stated.

"We're nothing without the glue, Mary."

"Great, I'm reduced to being something sticky. Oh, well, let's get this asshole and see what we can come up with."

**Barren Drive, West El Paso**

"It looks quiet," Knocker said to Cara. "The pickup isn't there."

"Doesn't mean that there's no one home though," she replied.

"One way to find out."

"You know that the general said to shoot

you if you got out of line, right?"

He gave her a weird smile that said he was going to do it shot or otherwise. "Yes."

"Shit." Cara reached for the door handle and opened her door. "Come on then, Limey."

The SAS man smiled knowingly as he opened his own door. "Limey. I like that."

"I thought you would," she said as she took out her M17.

They crossed the street and hurried through a broken gate then along the path towards a white house which was in need of a couple of coats of paint. The porch was covered with junk like most of the other rundown houses on the same street.

"Reaper Two, what are you doing?" Ferrero asked over Cara's comms.

"Having a look to see if there's anyone at home."

"You were told to hold position until the others arrived."

"It's all quiet. I'm reasonably sure that there's nobody here."

"I don't like it. Be careful."

"Copy that."

She looked at Knocker and nodded. The SAS man tried the door and it opened with an almost mute snick. He went through the opening with practiced ease as he'd done so many times before when making breaches. He swept the hallway inside and took the first doorway on his left. It led to the living room. He swept that and apart from a holey sofa, a television, and stained carpet, he found it clear. Behind him Cara moved further along the hallway and took the next doorway on the left. It was a bedroom with a single bed and nothing else.

Cara backed out of it and moved further along the hallway to the next door. It was locked when she tried it, so she gave it a solid kick. It flew back, splintering the jamb and punched a hole in the drywall when the knob slammed into it.

The room was clear.

Meanwhile Knocker had moved from the living room into the open plan kitchen where he found the body of Chet on the kitchen floor, his feet poking out from behind an island. "Cara! I've got our man here."

She entered the kitchen. "Falomo?"

"No, Chet. The guy who lives here."

Cara looked down at the body and saw the hole in his head from where he'd been shot. The telltale marks around it told her the shooter had been close. She said into her comms. "Zero, Reaper Two. Our target is down, I say again, our target is down. He was dead when we got here. Shot up close."

"Read you Lima Charlie, Reaper Two. Any sign of our HVT?"

"Negative."

"Roger. Secure and wait for the rest of the team. Out."

"Look at this," Knocker said pointing at papers on the island. Cara stared at the one on top of the pile then realized that she should be looking at the bigger one below it. Blueprints.

She swept the paper on top away and picked the larger one up. She looked at the top right corner and read the title. El Paso Central Mall Complex. On the left side about halfway down was a faint circle. Cara frowned and looked back at the island. Another, smaller sheet caught her eye. She picked it up and caught her breath. It was the air-conditioning system. "He's going to put it through the air-conditioning system."

"Not the whole lot he isn't. Be damn impossible," Knocker told her. "A small amount, yes. It would still have the desired effect."

"So, the rest of it still has to be here somewhere. Or somewhere close."

"Maybe."

"Zero? Reaper Two."

"Go ahead, Reaper Two."

"Zero, we've found plans for the El Paso Central Mall Complex along with the air-conditioning system. It looks like he's going to try and disperse some of it there."

"What about the rest, Reaper Two?"

"No sign of it but we'll have another look around."

"Negative. Get over to the mall. I'll divert Reaper and the others. El Paso PD can search the house."

"Roger that. We're on our way."

### El Paso Central Mall

They all met up in the parking lot which was full of vehicles of every description. Kane took one look at them all and shook his head. "If Falomo lets that stuff loose in there we're in deep trouble."

Cara nodded as she took the tactical vest he offered her. She put it on and then took the HK416. "Let's hope we can shut him down before he does."

"Have you got the blueprints?"

She laid them out on the hood of the SUV and the team gathered around. "There are three main exits," Cara pointed out. "But even more emergency ones."

Kane looked up and motioned to a police officer who was starting to gather men in the lot. He jogged over and stopped next to the Team

Reaper commander. Kane said, "I need police at every exit on this building. Go."

"Yes, sir."

"If we split up into teams of two and sweep towards the basement where the AC is, we might get lucky. We'll have to push hard and fast though."

Kane was about to agree when gunfire rang out from within. "Shit. Everybody move. Axe with me. Carlos and Brick. Cara, you take Knocker. Go."

The team infiltrated the mall against the crush of shoppers coming the other way who were guided by police and security guards. At first it was almost impossible to get through but once inside they moved to a wall and slid along it to stay out of the human wave.

Cara said, "Reaper Two and Six are inside."

"Three and Five are good."

"One and Four are in."

More gunfire rang out and cries of alarm echoed throughout the food hall ahead. "What are they shooting at?" Cara asked. "Slick can you see what's going on?"

"There are three shooters in the food hall ahead of you, Reaper Two."

"I don't get it. Why, if he plans to release it here and kill as many as possible? Unless …"

"What is it, Reaper Two?" Ferrero asked.

"He's not here, Zero. It's a diversion and we fell for it. The blueprints at the house were a plant to throw us off."

"How do you know?" Ferrero asked.

"I just do. I feel it. Why would he start shooting people when he wants to release the anthrax and get as many people as possible?"

"What's his target then?"

A bullet ricocheted from the wall where Cara was standing. "That's for you to work out. Contact front!"

The 416 came up and she tried to find a target through the throng. Cursing under her breath she called to Knocker, "I can't see a damned thing."

"Up the stairs," he called back. "Follow me."

Cara followed him to an escalator, and he started to run up the upward one. The downward one was packed with a heaving mass of panicked people. Once he'd reached the landing the SAS man hurried across to the railing and looked down. "There they are."

Cara joined him and saw the three shooters holding what looked to be AR-15s. On the floor there were four bodies and one of those had the uniform of a security guard. The others were two men and a woman, no doubt shoppers.

"What do you want to do?" Knocker asked.

"Put them down before they can kill anyone else."

They sighted on the shooters and Cara was the first to fire. Two bullets from her 416 crashed into the first shooter's chest at a downward angle from right to left. He collapsed, the weapon he held clattering to the tiled floor.

Beside her Cara heard Knocker's weapon fire twice and a second shooter went down. The third killer reacted instantly to his comrades' deaths. He swung his AR upwards and without aiming fired at Cara and Knocker. The bullets cracked around them and forced them to pull back from the rail. With them out of sight the third shooter moved out of the open.

The two operators moved back to the rail and looked down. Their target was gone. "Shit," the SAS man growled. "The wanker's gone."

"Back down, follow me."

They ran toward the escalator. As they went Cara made a report. "Zero, we have our civilians and two shooters down on the ground floor. One shooter is still active. In pursuit, out."

"Good copy, Reaper Two."

"Reaper Two, this is One. We're moving towards your position."

"Copy. Be aware that he's armed with an AR-15."

"Roger that."

They hit the ground floor and turned left out into the food court. Screams of panic sounded further along to their right and Cara could see a crowd of civilians rapidly dispersing. Parting like Moses did the Red Sea and, in the middle, stood the third shooter who now had a hostage. A young woman no older than twenty.

"There, Knocker," Cara blurted out. "The asshole has a hostage."

With weapons raised they both walked toward the killer, their sights not wavering. When he saw them approach, the shooter dropped the AR and pulled a handgun from his belt. He placed it against the hostage's head. "Stay back or I'll fucking kill her. Just see if I don't."

"Put the gun down. It's over. There's no-where else to go."

"I can take him," Knocker whispered into his comms.

"No, we need to know where Falomo is."

"Back off," the man screeched.

He was African and judging by his accent he'd not been in the US long.

"Where's Abadi Falomo?" Cara called out.

"You will not stop him."

"Let the girl go and we can talk."

"No! Put your guns down or I will kill her."

Cara glanced at the young woman. Her eyes

were full of tears as she struggled to get free. Her lips mouthed silent pleas for help.

"If you kill her, I'm going to kill you," Cara said plainly. "And if I don't, my friend here will. Let the girl go and tell us where Falomo is."

"Why? You will let me go? Huh?"

"We'll let you live."

"No, you let me go."

"There's no coming back from what you've done," Cara told him. "The best you can hope for is to walk out of here alive."

Suddenly the killer's expression changed, and a look of resignation swept across it. But just as rapidly the expression changed again, and a snarl exploded from his lips. He was going to kill the girl.

Knocker fired. The 5.56 round from the 416 punched into the killer's forehead and his head snapped back. The risk that the killer would reflexively jerk the trigger on the handgun was enormous. But the SAS man figured that the hostage was dead one way or the other. So, he took the shot.

The killer dropped to the floor, the unfired handgun beside him when it spilled from his grip. The hostage raced forward, and Cara scooped her up in her arms, holding her close. She looked across at Knocker who smiled at her.

"Zero? Reaper Two. Situation has been resolved. All shooters are down."

"Roger that, Reaper Two. Good to hear. Now we have another problem."

# CHAPTER 21

*Worldwide Drug Initiative HQ, El Paso*

"What do you mean it was all there?" Kane asked over his comms.

"I only know what El Paso PD told us, Reaper One," Ferrero said. "All of the cocaine was found in the basement."

"How did we miss that?" Cara asked.

"Exactly what I asked them. Apparently, there was a door hidden behind a rack in the closet."

"So, what is Falomo's endgame?" Kane asked.

"That's what we're trying to work out."

"What do you want us to do?" Kane asked.

"Return to base while we try to get on top of this. But at this time, we've got nothing. It's as though Falomo has given up and is in the wind."

"Do you believe that?"

"Not for a second. Out."

Ferrero walked over to where Swift worked on his computer, trying to track down the elusive terrorist. "Do you have anything?"

"Nothing. The guy is a ghost."

"Don't tell me that. He's out there somewhere."

"I'm trying but I'm coming up empty."

"To give up on his plan like he has is out of the ordinary. There must be a stronger pull out there somewhere. Maybe he's skipped the in-between and jumped to the endgame. Dig into his past. We know what happened in his past, see if the answer lies there. Dig like you've never dug before, Slick."

Thurston appeared at Ferrero's shoulder. "Anything?"

"Not yet."

"At least we got the drugs."

"Yes, but I want that bastard," Ferrero hissed.

### El Paso, Texas

Admiral Nesbit Neale sipped his glass of whiskey and watched as more guests arrived for his seventieth birthday celebrations. It was times like this he wished he could disappear upstairs

with the bottle and enjoy the quiet. Or escape
to sea on a carrier where he was the boss, not
that nagging old biddy who—

"Caught you," a feminine voice said from
behind him.

Neale rolled his eyes and ground his teeth
together. Fuck it! "Have to get up early before
one can trick you, dear."

"You know what the doctor said about alcohol, Nesbit," Florence Neale admonished her
husband. "No more."

"Damn it, woman—"

"Stop, Nesbit. I'm not one of your sailors. I'm
your wife and I'll be treated as such."

Florence was the same age as Neale and the
two had been married for the past forty years,
most of which he'd been at sea for. Thank
Christ.

"Go and greet our new guests, Nesbit and
then see what's keeping the waiters with their
fresh bottles of champagne."

"Yes, dear."

"And no drinking the stuff."

"Wouldn't touch it if I was fucking dead," he
muttered.

"Pardon?"

"Nothing, dear, just mumbling to myself."

"I thought so. When you find out about
the champagne let me know, will you? I'll be

talking to Wendy Smythe."

"Of course, you will."

"What was that?"

"I said I sure will."

"Thank you."

"God put me on a ship and sink it," Neale muttered.

He greeted the new arrivals, former captain, Walter Brandt and his wife Emily. Brandt had served under Neale on the USS Nevada. Plus, former Lieutenant Commander Ike Trent, he'd served under Neale on the USS Abraham Lincoln. Shit, were they all former? He looked around the room and saw it filled with gray heads. Yes, they were all old and past their prime just like he was.

"Give me a damned drink."

Neale was about to push his way through the door into the kitchen when a heavily accented voice from behind him said, "Excuse me, Admiral, someone has just told me that one of the toilets is backed up."

Neale turned and ran a hostile gaze over the man who stood before him. "Damn it. Which one?"

"The one upstairs."

"Where are you from?"

"Sir?"

"Where are you from? You're not American.

Not with that accent."

"I'm from Nigeria."

"Refugee, are you?"

Stark white teeth showed against the waiter's dark skin. "Yes, sir."

Neale grunted and headed towards the stairs under the gaze of the waiter. He stomped up them one at a time, his right hip feeling every riser. He muttered angrily once more and decided to raid the liquor cabinet in his den while he was up there.

On making the landing, he walked along the hallway until he reached the bathroom. When he opened the door and saw nothing—no mess, no water, no anything—Neale shrugged. Maybe the waiter got it mixed up and the downstairs toilet was backed up. He was about to turn back when a hand planted in the middle of his back and shoved him hard. The admiral spilled forward onto the tiles, his legs unable to keep up with his torso. His outstretched hands stopped him from cracking his head on the floor but only just.

The door slammed behind him and Neale turned his head to look around. Standing in front of the closed door was the waiter from downstairs.

"What the hell do you think you're doing?" Neale growled more from shock than anything.

"I'm here for you, Admiral," Falomo stated. "For your life."

"What do you mean?" Neale asked, sitting down unsure if he could get up even if he wanted too. "Do I know you?"

"The Gulf of Guinea. In nineteen ninety-eight you authorized a strike on some pirates based on the Nigerian coast."

The admiral tried to keep his face blank, but his eyes gave him away. "I see you do remember. I was a young boy then. I watched my father die and lost my mother, my whole family. Killed by you."

"I had nothing to do with it," Neale snapped.

"Liar!" Falomo roared and ripped his shirt open.

Neale's eyes grew wide as he realized what it was that the ISWA leader was wearing. A suicide vest. The man had come here to kill him and most probably half of the people downstairs by the look of the amount of explosive he had in it.

Neale swallowed. "You want me, fine, but don't kill anyone else."

"Why not, you're all the same imperialists. You think you own the world. I would not be surprised if some of the men downstairs were with you on the carrier that day."

He was right. There were at least four. "No.

No one else."

"You are lying again."

"No, I'm not."

"I can see it in your eyes."

"Fuck you," Neale hissed, realizing there was nothing he could do or say which would stop Falomo.

The smile came back to Falomo's face. The broad smile which showed his stark white teeth. "No. Fu—"

### Worldwide Drug Initiative HQ, El Paso

"Luis, the airwaves have just gone nuts. There's reports of an explosion in suburban east El Paso."

"Is it a house or what?" Ferrero demanded.

Out of the corner of his eye, the operations commander saw Thurston approach. "What's going on?"

"Explosion in east El Paso."

"You think it's him?"

"Too much of a coincidence not to be."

"Sir," Swift said interrupting, "the place where the explosion happened was a residence. It belonged to an Admiral Nesbit Neale retired."

"Christ."

"That's not all, sir. I looked into his record. Cross-referenced it with Nigeria, and it turns out that he was the leader of the taskforce which raided a pirate camp back in ninety-eight. I can't confirm it at the moment but…"

Ferrero nodded. "I think I can put the pieces together."

"Do you want me to let the team know so they can relocate? Maybe get a lead."

Ferrero shook his head. "No, let them come home. It's over."

"But he'll get away," Swift protested.

"No, he won't. This was his end game. He couldn't get rid of the drugs, so he cut straight to the end. There was no getting away this time. Gather what intel you can and have it for me later."

"Yes, sir."

Ferrero turned and looked at Thurston. "Sometimes…"

She nodded knowing what he was going to say. "Yes, sometimes the bad guys win. We can't do everything. If we could we'd be super-heroes."

"It's still shit, though."

"Yes, it is."

**2 Days Later**

"Hey, Limey, you ready to go?" Axe called over to Knocker.

The SAS man's gaze settled on Cara and he

said, "You've been teaching him, I see."

She smiled. "Poor sod was out of his depth."

Knocker's smile broadened. "You too?"

"What can I say?"

He looked at Kane who stood beside her. "What about you?"

The Team Reaper commander spread his arms in a helpless gesture. "I have trouble speaking American."

Knocker held out his hand. "Great working with you. Shame it went all to pot at the end."

Kane grinned and shook his hand. "Can't win them all. Maybe we'll cross paths again soon."

"You ever need any help, look me up."

"I'll do that."

He turned to Cara. "And you, Princess. You are something in a kerfuffle."

She raised an eyebrow at him.

"All right, You're something special in a fight. I'd go to war with you anytime."

"Same here, Limey."

He embraced her and kissed her cheek. "If you're ever in the UK look me up."

"We'll go to the pub and have a beer."

Knocker smiled again. "You impress me all the time."

Then he turned to the others. "Thanks for everything. Been a pleasure. You're all fucking crazy, but I guess that's what makes you special."

"You're calling us crazy?" Thurston asked.

He winked at her. "You want to get a beer before I leave?"

"The door is that way, Mucker," Thurston said pointing towards it.

"Well what do you know, the woman loves me."

"Get out of here."

Knocker took up his kit and started towards the door. When he drew level with Axe the big ex-recon marine asked him, "What were you all saying back there?"

Knocker slapped him on the back. "My friend, I'll explain everything when we get to the car."

Cara looked at Kane after the pair had disappeared. "He's going to return even more confused than when he left."

"Without a doubt, my dear Watson. Without a doubt."

A LOOK AT: KILL THEORY

TEAM REAPER 11

## TEAM REAPER IS IN A FIGHT FOR THEIR LIVES!

One by one, the top officials of US anti-drug agencies are targeted for murder. A cartel hit squad is running free in Washington, DC, and racking up a body count that sends shock waves through federal law enforcement.

Team Reaper must stop the killings, but John Kane begins to suspect a web of corruption that extends to the highest levels of the government. The assignment against the cartel hit team is compromised from the start, and soon Team Reaper is under attack. With Kane and his crew cut off from support, and seemingly disavowed from the very government they serve, the team is forced to go rogue, scorching the earth to find out who betrayed them, why, and discover who's truly behind the killings...

The enemy sees a blurred line between good and evil; Team Reaper will make it crystal clear.

COMING MARCH 2020

# ABOUT THE AUTHOR

A relative newcomer to the world of writing, Brent Towns self-published his first book, a western, in 2015. Last Stand in Sanctuary took him two years to write. His first hardcover book, a Black Horse Western, was published the following year.

Since then, he has written a further 26 western stories, including some in collaboration with British western author, Ben Bridges.

Also, he has written the novelization to the upcoming 2019 movie from One-Eyed Horse Productions, titled, Bill Tilghman and the Outlaws. Not bad for an Australian author, he thinks.

Brent Towns has also scripted three Commando Comics with another two to come.

He says, "The obvious next step for me was to venture into the world of men's action/adventure/thriller stories. Thus, Team Reaper was born."

For more information:
https://wolfpackpublishing.com/brent-towns/